'Look beyond the frontispiece!'

Also available:

The Golden Sword

(The Camelot Inheritance ~ Book 1)

The Time Smugglers

(The Camelot Inheritance ~ Book 2)

Written by Rosie Morgan

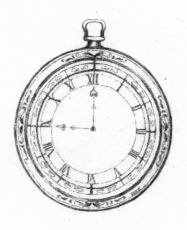

~ When the past and present collide ~

Illustrations by Rosie Morgan

With those of Dragon by Helen Blenkhorn

(Dragon is extremely pleased with Helen's illustrations,
and says that she can draw him whenever she wants.)

Cover by Katie Stewart

~ Magic Owl Design ~

~ For Charles and Jessica-Rose ~
My rather wonderful and inspirational children

For the past with the present and future entwine,
Providing the perfect circle of time.

Contents

Map of Cornwall – or Kernow

From Pendrym

to the Smugglers Way

Bodmin Moor

The Jollys' Cottage

The Lake

Lyskeret

The Smugglers' Way

Dywana's Cottgae

Pendrym

Porth Talant

Porth Pyra

Lemayne Island

Prologue

A year ago Arthur Penhaligon was just a normal teenager; he didn't believe in magic, or time travel, or shape-shifting animals. Although to be fair to him, not many people do.

Few people have any idea that there may be another world waiting for them outside their front door; and until that sunny morning last summer, Arthur didn't either. Anyway, his life was too full of school, skateboarding and hanging out with friends to give anything so impossible even a passing thought.

So his shock when he encountered the sinister Crow Man, who could summon storms at will, was understandable; but to then discover that he had somehow acquired *another* enemy, in the shape of the pale and malevolent stranger known as Hagarawall... well, anybody would start to worry!

But, much to his relief, Arthur found that this strange world wasn't going to be *all* bad because within a couple of days he'd met Michael and Angela Jolly, (who were both a bit weird and mystical but definitely on his side); and then Bedivere, a (supposedly) long-dead knight. While right from the outset there'd been Cathe, the shape-shifting cat, who'd made it very clear that Arthur's cause was his cause.

So by the time Arthur and his friends, Nick, Tamar and Gawain, were assembled together on a moonlit hill - along with a medieval knight and a legendary sword - he was prepared to admit that there might be rather more to life than just skateboarding and computers.

Almost willing to accept his birthright as Cornwall's Guardian. Even ready to be knighted by that famous sword, Excalibur... which is precisely what happened.

(However before we move on, perhaps it should be noted that Arthur was blissfully unaware of the careful monitoring of these events by a couple of overworked time travellers, known as the Watchers. And that these Watchers, Viatoris and Servo, were directed by the illusive Writer - a woman who could easily be mistaken for a rather strict head teacher.)

...

But, of course, that was last year.

Since then life has been remarkably quiet. Nothing in the least bit unusual has happened. It's just been school and homework. (Isn't that typical? You've finally got used to ancient knights and shape-shifting animals and you're gearing yourself up for the next magical event, when it all comes to a grinding halt.) However Arthur and his friends might not have to wait too much longer before the magic begins to stir itself again.

They don't know it yet, but both on land and at sea, Cornwall's enemies and allies are beginning to gather.

On a Cornish cliff path a tiny, green-stone dragon stretches a claw; while in a churchyard high above a sheltered cove a carved angel tests his wings. And out at sea an emerald pocket watch chimes once... and slips through time.

The invisible Watchers are in place and the mysterious Writer is ready.

However the Crow Man is also prepared, determined to seize power from his sworn enemy – Arthur Penhaligon.

The stage is set. Let Act Two commence.

Comero weeth – take care.

Chapter 1

~ The enemy returns ~

The seal pushed himself off the rocks and slid into the sea. Moments later he emerged beneath the creaking hull of the ship, its tall masts swaying in rhythm with the rise and fall of the water. The animal swam from stern to bow before coming to rest below the prow.

Above the seal a figure leant over the rail, surveying the cliffs rising up from the water's edge. His gaze was drawn towards a tiny hamlet nestling in a wooded valley.

A light flickered in a cottage window, a door opened and snatches of conversation escaped into the night. The man leant further forward, straining to catch the words, but was interrupted by a shout from somewhere deep inside the ship.

He turned, irritated, and after casting a quick look back towards the cottage disappeared from his watch. Below him, the sea-hidden spy vanished beneath the waves as silently as he'd arrived.

The Guardians' enemies were gathering.

. . .

'Are you staying with your aunt all summer?' Tamar asked.

'Dunno, depends how long Mum and Dad are away I suppose,' Arthur replied.

'Well, it's a pretty cool place to stay,' Nick said. 'It's great having the beach at the end of the garden.'

Arthur, watching a vapour trail stretch across the wide blue sky, nodded agreeing.

The three of them were sitting on a hillside above a secluded bay with fields and woods running down to the sea. Sheep dotted the steep, green land behind them and a tractor chugged along the brow of the hill. Arthur knew that it was almost ideal, and it would have been if it weren't for that prickle of apprehension stubbornly lodged between his shoulder blades.

Although they were unaware of it they made an interesting trio, with Tamar and her waist-length black hair, and the two boys, one blond and the other dark haired.

However his appearance, or anyone else's, was the last thing on Arthur's mind because he was sure that something was wrong.

He gazed at the view - and wondered.

'Arthur, is Gawain coming over?' Tamar asked. 'I thought you said that he'd be here.'

'Yeah,' Nick said, 'when I spoke to him he told me that he was going to have time off today.'

But Arthur was temporarily distracted by a movement on the beach below them, 'What?'

Squinting into the sun, he narrowed his eyes and focused on the rocks rearing up at the edge of the beach. He thought that he'd glimpsed a familiar figure disappear behind them moments before.

'Gawain,' Nick repeated, 'he should be here.'

'Oh… yeah,' Arthur replied, watching the rocks. He had a feeling that the person had been wearing a long coat and a wide-brimmed hat, the preferred clothing of the Crow Man. Yet as fast as the idea took shape he banished it. Surely there was no way that his old enemy could be here, in Porth Talant?

'Arthur,' Tamar exclaimed impatiently, 'you're not listening to a word we're saying!'

He pulled himself back. 'Oh right, Gawain… no, he can't come. He has to help out in his uncle's shop today.'

Gawain was the fourth of the Guardians. In the last year they'd spent a lot of time together. After all, who else would understand the strange world they'd been plunged into on that mysterious night when they'd been made Guardians of Cornwall? As a result they really had become the four musketeers, as Nick had called them, bonded by magic and duty. It wasn't that they consciously tried to exclude other people; it was just easier when it was the four of them – and it felt safer.

'That's tough, I bet he's fed up,' Nick said, fiddling with a tiny, silver sword hanging from a chain around his neck, but already his grasshopper mind had moved on. 'Hey, do you guys still keep your swords on all the time?'

Tamar nodded as she toyed with the sword and chain that she'd been given, 'I do.'

Arthur tore his gaze away from the rocks, 'Remember what Michael said? He told us we *had* to wear them all the time.'

'Yeah,' Nick said, 'but none of us really know what they're for, *and* it's been a whole year since we saw him.' He paused, 'Everything's been so.... normal, I'm beginning to wonder if anything interesting will ever happen!'

They thought about that night a year ago, its magic and their commissioning, but Nick was right, nothing even slightly unusual had happened since then.

Together they contemplated the view laid out in front of them: a seagull idly drifting high above the bay, cotton-wool clouds dotting the blue sky and waves lapping on the soft, Cornish sand. Looking at all of this it was hard to believe that anything *could* happen.

Arthur stretched and stroked Lightning, his constant canine companion of the last year, and looked at the hill behind him. He watched the tractor slow as it approached the gate and saw the farmer jump down to open it.

He was so absorbed, wondering whether it was Farmer Martin or one of his sons, that he didn't notice the tall, long-limbed figure reappear and scramble over the rocks at the edge of the beach, accompanied by a midnight-feathered bird.

Neither did he see the man grab a piece of driftwood lying on the sand and weigh it thoughtfully in his hand before disappearing behind a rocky outcrop.

In the bay below them a sun-hatted toddler was busy examining a rock pool and further out to sea yachts glided, while towards the shore people swam and paddled.

It was a picture-perfect scene.

But an instant later their peace was shattered by Tamar grabbing the chain hanging around her neck and exclaiming, 'Ow, my sword – it's *freezing*!'

'So's mine!' Nick said, peering curiously at the tiny silver object he was holding.

And Arthur had promptly grasped his chain, swinging the sword away from his neck, because his too was ice-cold.

They looked at each other, surely this had to be more than just a coincidence. And immediately Arthur was reminded of the stones left for him by the Crow Man the previous year - because they'd done this too. Whenever anything, or anyone, dangerous had been nearby the stones had reacted. Their temperature had dropped just like this.

He looked down to the beach and up to the hills but he couldn't see anything different. He could still hear the tractor and see the children playing on the sand, but he'd learnt that appearances could be deceptive.

It looked like the waiting that Nick had been complaining about might be finally over.

'Be careful what you wish for!' he muttered to himself.

Suddenly Lightning sat up, wide awake.

'Hey boy, can you feel it too?' Arthur asked.

It was obvious that something had grabbed the dog's attention because by now he was standing with every muscle tensed, concentrating on the beach at a point where the cliff jutted out separating this bay from its neighbour.

The only way of getting to the other bay was over the jagged rocks, but before Arthur was able to stop him Lightning had taken off.

'Lightning!'

But the dog was deaf to his call and was already at the base of the cliff, slithering and sliding over the treacherous rocks, determined to reach the neighbouring bay.

'Lightning, come back!'

For a split second Arthur stood undecided as to whether to follow but this was so out of character that he knew something must be wrong.

'Come on!' he yelled over his shoulder to his friends, and soon all three were racing down the hill towards the beach. None of them had time to see a dark bird, high in the sky above them, or a pair of black eyes surveying their progress from the water at the edge of the rocks. But they all heard the barking, the yelp, and the sudden silence.

They scrabbled around the base of the cliff, splashing through the rock pools and over the slimy seaweed. Rounding the corner they slid down the rocks to the deserted beach and Arthur's stomach flipped because a black and white shape was lying at the water's edge. Blood was seeping from the body, staining the sand rose-pink and running in tiny rivulets to mingle with the sea.

'Lightning!' Arthur's shout echoed off the surrounding cliffs.

He rushed to where the dog lay and leant over to stroke him but there was no reaction. Frantically he searched the animal's body, trying to find where he was injured. His hand travelled over Lightning's silky back and up towards his head to find blood bubbling from a deep gash in the dog's skull.

Nick and Tamar were just behind Arthur but it took a few moments before the realisation hit them that the limp form on the sand was Arthur's dog. They looked on, shocked, as Arthur talked to Lightning, willing him to move and oblivious to the waves inching their way up the beach as the tide hurried in.

'Who did this to you?' Arthur murmured as he stroked Lightning's still body. He felt sick as a dull dread began to take hold. He watched as scarlet beads of the dog's blood dribbled out of the open wound, and as Lightning's breathing became lighter with every, tiny breath. Tears misted his vision. He couldn't believe that this dog, which barely ever left his side, was dying in front of him and that there was nothing he could do to save him.

But the tide wouldn't stop for anyone. The water was creeping in, crawling up the beach and lapping around Nick's feet. Arthur's friend glanced up from watching Lightning to find the sea edging up the sand, and knew that it would only take a few more minutes for them to be completely stranded. There was no way out of the bay other than over the rocks - and soon they'd be submerged. They had to get out before they were trapped.

'Arthur,' Nick said quietly, 'the tide's coming in ...'

Tamar looked at the fast-rising water and understood what Nick was talking about but she shook her head. She knew that there was no way that Arthur would leave Lightning - and she wasn't about to give up on him either.

'There must be someone who can help,' she said desperately, and then a thought struck her. 'I know! Hang on a minute ...' and rummaging in her bag she pulled out her phone.

'You can't get a signal down here,' Nick stated gently, pointing to the cliffs high above them.

Tamar's face fell. 'Oh no, I'd forgotten that.'

She twisted her hair through her fingers as she thought and then her face lit up. Reaching into her bag, she pulled out her towel and thrust one end at Nick, 'We can roll him onto this, it's easily big enough, and then we can take him back.'

'There's no way we can carry him over those rocks,' Nick protested. 'They're really slippery and he's a big dog, he'll be too heavy.'

Holding her end of the towel she nodded towards Arthur, 'Come on Nick, we've *got* to try.'

Nick looked at their friend and at the incoming water and knew that Tamar was right, it was their only option.

'Okay,' he sighed. 'Come on then, we'll give it a go.'

Arthur looked up as Nick and Tamar advanced. He understood what his friends were doing but in his heart he knew that they were fighting against the odds. Lightning was slipping away in front of his eyes. However he continued to talk quietly to his dog, willing him to hang on long enough to get him to help. Tamar tucked the top end of the towel under Lightning's head, positioning it so that it could be pulled under his body, while Nick and Arthur stood either side of the dog ready to lift him.

They were so caught up in their efforts that none of them noticed the prow of a rowing boat nudge into view around the rocks until a voice startled them.

'Could you be doin' with some help?'

Sitting in the boat a little way off the shore was a fisherman, with his navy-blue sailing cap pushed to the back of his head and his shirt sleeves rolled up. He was leaning forward, resting on his oars, casually dipping one into the water whenever he needed to maintain the boat's position.

'You got trouble with your dog, boy?'

Arthur nodded. He couldn't bring himself to speak.

The fisherman looked around, casting his eyes over the cliffs and the woods above them, before rowing the boat further in and stepping over the side. Without a word he handed Nick a rope tethered to the boat's prow and bent down beside Lightning's body, then he gently ran his hands over the animal's head and side.

He grunted, "e be in a bad way, but he's not done for.'

And then in one deft movement he was gathering the dog up in his arms, lifting him over the side of the boat and setting him gently down on the boards.

'Come on,' he said to Arthur and his friends. 'In you get.'

Arthur snapped out of his reverie and scrambled after the fisherman. He sat on the boards of the boat cradling Lightning's head in his lap, while Tamar and Nick grabbed their bags and hurried after him. The minute they were on board the fisherman pushed the boat away from the shore and started rowing. Once they were further out he looked up at the tree-screened cliffs and frowned.

High on the cliff path, a crow flapped lazily above a man wearing a long, dark coat and a wide-brimmed hat. He was standing completely still, observing the progress of the little boat and making no effort to hide; in fact it was almost as if he was waiting to be seen. And indeed, the moment that he caught the fisherman's eye he lifted up a thick branch to show him something glistening on the end of the wood.

Slowly, and very deliberately, the man drew his finger along it and held it up for the fisherman to see.

The end of his finger was scarlet, the colour of blood; Lightning's blood.

The fisherman's face darkened and his frown deepened, but he said nothing to his passengers as the man on the cliff raised his hat and turned away.

...

Above the bay a sudden breeze swept up a pile of dead leaves and set the flowers in the hedges trembling. A second later two figures stepped out of the shadows, glanced at one another and then at the scene in front of them.

Both men were slightly blurred at the edges, just a little out of focus, because both of them had been pulled from other centuries and places.

They were the Watchers, Viatoris and Servo, time-travellers who'd been summoned to Cornwall to observe Arthur and the other Guardians. They'd arrived at the moment that the fisherman had become the unwilling witness to the method of Lightning's injury. They too had seen the bloodied branch.

One said, 'So the Crow Man has arrived and already he has drawn blood!'

His companion nodded grimly. 'He will be wanting revenge, Servo.'

'Revenge? But for what?'

'For the death of Matearnas.'

'Ah, of course, the self-proclaimed Queen of Cornwall.'

Viatoris nodded, 'Sadly, the Crow Man – Brane - persists in blaming young Arthur for her death.'

The Watchers continued to study the activity below them: the man on the cliff path, and the fisherman rowing his passengers and the brutally injured dog to safety.

'The Rule states that we must never intervene,' one of the Watchers said, 'but at times it is a hard command to follow.'

They were quiet as they contemplated their commission: to observe the progress of those assigned to them - but never to interfere.

His companion nodded, sighing, 'So, Servo, you have come from Watching your other charge in Egypt?'

'I have, Viatoris. He does well. And you?'

'Ah, I have been given an assignment in Italy,' the Watcher was on the point of going into more detail when a movement out at sea stopped him. A sailing ship had appeared from behind a small island that lay a mile or two out from the mainland. It was a magnificent vessel, fully rigged and moving smoothly across the water, which wouldn't have been particularly unusual except for the complete lack of even the smallest breeze. The wind that had earlier powered the yachts in the bay had dropped leaving the air still and heavy, yet the ship's sails still billowed.

Viatoris plunged his hand into his shirt pocket and pulled out a velvet drawstring bag. He extracted a small, leather case, pressed the clasp, took out a compass and pointed it out to sea. The face of the compass was constructed differently to most others in that there was an inner, solid circle with an ornate needle at its centre, surrounded by a separate ring which could move independently. Together the Watchers studied it as the needle came to life.

The outer ring of the compass was decorated with intricate pictures. On one side brightly painted butterflies and miniscule birds flew above exotic flowers, while on the opposite edge grey and black flowers grew and withered.

Viatoris tilted the compass and the needle wobbled and spun until it was pointing to the tall-masted ship as it sailed across the bay. Then the outer circle of the compass began to rotate.

The Watchers waited as the decorated ring made a few rotations before finally slowing to a halt to leave the needle pointing towards the ship while resting on a black and dying flower. It appeared that the device was severely affected by its findings because the glass of the compass had started to mist over and the needle had begun to quiver.

'It is rare for her to react like this. Look how she trembles!' said Viatoris.

They watched as the needle rocked and shook.

The owner of the compass shook his head and pulled the leather case out of his pocket. With infinite care he opened the lid, placed the device inside and clicked the gold clasp shut. Then he pushed the case into the velvet pouch and tucked it into his shirt pocket, close to his chest.

'So their enemies are assembling,' he said.

The sailing ship continued on its voyage across the bay, eventually disappearing behind the finger of land that separated Porth Talant from its neighbouring village.

The Watchers turned their attention to the little rowing boat edging around the rocks below them with its precious cargo on board, and followed it as its owner steered it towards Porth Talant. It wasn't many minutes before it, too, had disappeared from their view.

Once it had gone both Watchers relaxed, certain that their charges would be safe, for now. Then Servo, dressed as a keen walker complete with woolly hat and walking boots, turned to Viatoris. He looked him up and down, taking in his companion's cloak and shoes which looked suspiciously like those of a court jester, and started to smile.

But before he could make a comment, Viatoris said, 'I have come from Watching the young Leonardo da Vinci in Italy, five hundred years from here. The fashion of that time demands this ridiculous footwear.'

He hauled a bag from the bushes with a flourish, 'But I am prepared!' And with that he proceeded to pull out a cap, a stripy pullover and a pair of scruffy jeans. He had the air of an 'A' class student. In anyone else it would be described as smug. But his smile faded as he searched deep inside the bag because his disguise as a fisherman was incomplete, he'd forgotten the boots.

Viatoris contemplated his footwear. There was no way a Cornish fisherman would be seen dead in those shoes. He sighed, they'd just have to do.

In an attempt to divert attention away from himself, he asked, 'So you still Watch Joseph, the Dreamer, in Egypt?'

Servo, the 'walker', nodded and was about to say something when the wooden masted ship, with its sails swollen by the non-existent wind, sailed back into view. This mission promised to be one of their more demanding projects. Overhead a dark-feathered bird circled. The men exchanged glances and picked up their bags before making their way along the cliff path.

There was Watching to be done.

...

Tamar scrutinised their rescuer as he steered the little boat around the rocks.

They'd never met but there was something familiar about him. She wondered where he lived… and how he'd managed to appear at just the right moment.

As if he'd heard her thoughts, he stated, 'I live in Porth Pyra, near your sister. My name's Jago Jolliff.'

Tamar frowned, how did he know about Morwenna, and that she was her sister?

He rowed, glancing at the cliffs and out to sea, and answered her unspoken question. 'Is there anyone in Porth Pyra who doesn't know Wenna?'

The fisherman smiled, 'We're on the same side, lass.'

Tamar looked at him sharply, wondering just how much he knew.

Again, without her needing to say a word, he said, 'An' young Arthur's staying in Porth Talant with his Aunt Dywana.'

For once Tamar was speechless. As fast as she thought something this man answered it, but at that moment her attention was diverted by a movement on the cliff path.

Two men, engaged in deep conversation, were walking side by side but as she watched they appeared to fade and melt into the shadows. Tamar leant forward, straining to get a better view, but they'd gone. She looked along the path – there was no sign of either man which was strange because she didn't know that there was another way off the cliff.

Nick, sorting their belongings, wasn't listening to the conversation.

He'd found a scrap of material which he'd picked up with Tamar's towel, it looked as though it could have been torn from a coat or something. Glancing towards Arthur and Lightning, he saw a tiny fragment of the same material at the corner of Lightning's mouth and an idea began to take shape.

As they rounded the rocks edging the bay of Porth Talant, a short round figure was running down the beach towards them with her skirts flapping.

'I've called the vet!' she was shouting. ''E'll be here dreckly.'

Tamar and Nick looked at each other. How had Dywana known they'd need a vet?

Their rescuer catching their puzzled glances, merely said, 'Not all of us need phones to call for help.'

He gave another pull on the oars, pushing the boat onto the beach, 'For some there's more direct means.'

He gently picked up the unconscious dog and stepped over the side of the boat.

'Come on boy,' he called to Arthur. 'Let's be making your dog comfortable afore the vet gets 'ere. You two alright to pull the boat up?'

Arthur clambered out and jogged after their rescuer, Lightning's survival was the only thing on his mind.

Nick and Tamar watched them make their way up the beach before wordlessly working together to pull the boat onto the sand, and out of the water.

Eventually Tamar turned to Nick and said, 'What d'you think he meant about there being more direct means?'

'No idea,' Nick shrugged. 'It's the sort of thing that Michael would have said, and I didn't always understand him! Come on, I want to see how Lightning's doing.'

They walked up the beach so preoccupied with all that had happened that neither of them noted a large ginger cat sitting on a stone wall, quietly observing them. Nor did they see it jump off the wall, its fur rippling from ginger to black and back to ginger again, as it followed them along the lane to Dywana's cottage.

Cathe was back.

Chapter 2

~ Stone Awakening ~

Arthur lay in his bed with his hands clasped behind his head, listening to the quiet rhythm of Lightning's breathing. He'd had to make a strong case for keeping his dog at the cottage. The vet had wanted to take him to the surgery for observation, but Arthur knew that Lightning's recovery depended on staying close to him. They hadn't been parted since that day last summer when the dog had mysteriously arrived at the café in Pendrym and adopted Arthur as his owner.

He rolled onto his side and peered over the edge of the bed at the sleeping animal and watched Lightning's paws twitch in his sleep.

'Wonder what you're chasing, boy.'

He sighed, 'No outings for you for a while, or you'll be shipped off to the vets quicker than you can say 'biscuits'.'

He lay back and watched the shadows chase each other across the ceiling, weaving in and out of the gnarled, wooden beams. The wind moaned, tugging the branches of the old oak tree which grew close to the cottage, its leaves scraping against the roof above his head.

Arthur sat up and stared into the darkness for a few seconds. Then carefully, so as not to disturb the dog, he swung his legs over Lightning's basket and crept across the worn carpet and pulled the curtains aside. A full moon lit the garden, illuminating the beach and the sea.

'It's no good,' he muttered to himself. 'There's no way I'm going to get back to sleep.'

Pulling on his sweatshirt, he quietly opened his door and padded downstairs. He knew that his aunt wouldn't mind if he helped himself to something to eat.

A lamp glowed on the windowsill in the kitchen, Dywana always left it on at night so that any lost fishermen would know where land lay. Beside it, a seal carved out of stone from the quarry on the moors, sparkled in the soft light. As usual Arthur stroked it as he passed and as usual, unseen by him, one eye blinked at his touch. He struck a match and lit a candle before turning around to survey the little kitchen.

A scrubbed pine table sat in the centre of the room surrounded by a selection of mismatched rickety chairs, while an old wooden dresser leant into the end wall. Along another wall, dusty shelves held a collection of coloured glass bottles and chipped stone jars: some were labelled with words that Arthur didn't recognise, while others had been left nameless. From time to time one of the bottles broke the silence by emitting a tiny blip as its contents heaved and sighed within their glass confines. For the first time in his life it occurred to Arthur to briefly wonder at what could be stored in this motley assortment of stone and glass, however his thoughts were soon back with Lightning and the day's events.

This was his second home, a refuge whenever he'd needed it, but his safe haven had been contaminated. Someone had harmed Lightning, maybe even tried to kill him. If it hadn't been for that fisherman happening to be there to rescue them, Lightning might not have made it. He pushed the thought away because life without his dog was unimaginable.

The stairs creaked and the door opened.

'Couldn't sleep then?' Arthur's aunt asked, knotting the belt around her dressing gown.

He shook his head.

Opening the larder door, she reached in and lifted out a large cake tin.

'Can't say I'm surprised, but Lightning's a strong animal. He'll be right as rain in a while,' his aunt said. 'How 'bout some cake?'

'That'd be great, thanks,' Arthur said. 'Yeah, I know what the vet said but I can't stop it going around in my head, Lightning running down that hill and over the rocks and disappearing. It was horrible. Part of me knew what I might find before I got to him, but when I got there and saw the blood… it was like a nightmare!'

Dywana opened a cupboard door, took out a couple of plates and cut a piece of chocolate cake, iced and covered with cherries. She pushed a plate towards him, then leant back against the dresser. Folding her arms she studied him thoughtfully. For a while she said nothing until she broke the silence with another question.

'Tell me Art, 'as anything happened with the swords?'

Arthur froze before slowly lifting his head to meet his aunt's gaze. The wind sighed as he said, 'I didn't think anyone else knew about them.'

'Not many of us do,' she acknowledged.

'But...'

'Your Great-Uncle Lance and I were friends. We shared many secrets hidden from those around us,' she stated, as if this explained everything. 'Still do,' she added quietly to herself.

Lance Penhaligon had given Arthur a model of an ancient knight when his great-nephew had been a small boy. That statue had played a pivotal role in the events of the previous summer.

'That's impossible, Great-Uncle Lance was really old!' Arthur exclaimed, thinking back to the last time he'd seen him.

Dywana smiled. 'That's very flattering Art, but you 'ave no idea of my age.'

Arthur looked at her, she didn't seem any older than his mum, apart from her long rope of silver hair, and yet if she'd been close to his great-uncle she must be a lot older. His world was beginning to shift again.

And then there was the painting of the knight. Why hadn't it occurred to him that it was just a little bit unusual to have such a large painting of a knight on a cottage kitchen wall?

The door creaked open and a large ginger cat strolled in, ambled over to the window and sprang onto the window sill. It tucked its tail around its body before turning to survey the garden and the beach beyond.

His aunt was watching him. 'You've grown up with all o' this around you Arthur, it's always been part of your life. Why should you see past what 'as always been there?'

Arthur turned and looked at the windowsill with its elegant feline occupant. Memories flooded back - of the

Yard last summer and his road lined with cats ruled by one, imposing creature.

'It's you, isn't it? You're the same cat,' he said.

He was fixed with a pair of green eyes and the animal started to purr, a deep rumbling purr, and Arthur was transported to the last time he'd seen it - at Michael and Angela's cottage.

Without taking his eyes off the animal, Arthur asked, 'How did he get here?'

'Cathe goes where 'e will, and wherever he's needed.'

'But when we went back to their cottage it was all shut up. It was totally deserted. There weren't any curtains hanging up, there were just cobwebs everywhere and all the furniture had gone!' Arthur exclaimed, watching the cat and remembering it curled up in front of Michael and Angela's fire. 'It looked like no one had lived there for years.'

'They also 'ave to go wherever they're needed,' Dywana said.

'But it was like it hadn't been used for at least a century!' Arthur protested, his shock at finding the Jollys' cottage locked and his own feeling of abandonment still as fresh as if it had been yesterday.

Dywana nodded, 'I know, t'is a difficult thing to understand, but their lives are not the lives of ordinary folks.'

She allowed a few moments to pass before she continued, 'So... the swords, have you noticed them gettin' cold?'

His hand automatically sought out the golden chain and sword given to him as chief Guardian and Guide. He'd got used to measuring his words, to being aware of who might hear a stray remark; however it was a huge relief to be able to talk about it with someone who clearly knew so much and was obviously on his side.

'Yes,' he said quietly. 'We all felt them go cold, very cold.'

He groaned. 'Lightning! That wasn't an accident, was it?'

She shook her head, 'I can't say for certain, but no, I think it was intended.'

A chilling possibility struck Arthur, 'The Crow Man, it's just the sort of thing he'd do.'

Dywana said nothing, allowing him to come to his own conclusions.

Arthur considered all the possibilities but he couldn't think of anyone else who would want to hurt, or even kill, his dog. His stomach churned at the thought of his old enemy having run him to ground here, in what he'd always thought of as the safest of places.

'He *must* know I'm here then.'

She sighed, 'I don't know for sure Art, but I wouldn't be surprised. You've been staying 'ere, off and on, for many years. Who can say how long 'e was watching you - even before last summer?'

A fog horn sounded and Arthur looked out of the window. A dense, grey mist rolled and swirled on the other side of the glass. He couldn't see anything; not even the gate which he knew was only a couple of steps outside the door.

'Where's that come from? It was clear a few moments ago.'

And immediately Dywana was by his side. 'Now, that *is* strange,' she said thoughtfully.

Together they inspected the fog pressing up against the glass, cloaking the cottage and the garden. Then the cat appeared to reach a decision and meowing, stood and stretched, and Arthur was once again fixed with that green-eyed gaze. It made a point of coming up close to him and rubbing his head against Arthur's arm before leaping off the window sill.

'When 'e does that he claims you as his,' Dywana stated.

They both watched the animal as it prowled across the kitchen before disappearing through the open door into the hall, and into the night.

'It's good to have something on my side.' Arthur muttered.

'Many are for you, Arthur Penhaligon,' Dywana said firmly. 'Remember your knighting? Remember 'ow many gathered together to witness their Guardian, their Guide, be knighted? Never forget that!'

Arthur didn't notice the knight in the painting nod once in agreement, but Dywana, catching the movement out of the corner of her eye, smiled.

. . .

On the cliff, high above the cottage and the sheltered cove, a shape stepped back into the shadows of an ancient church tower. He stood perfectly still, camouflaged by the grey mist, and congratulated himself on his choice of clothing. Servo adjusted his woolly hat and waited. Two other figures rounded the corner at the bottom of the path which led up and into the churchyard. Quiet voices carried on the night air. Snippets of conversation, one male and the other female.

The Watcher could just make out the woman's face as she turned to her companion, showing him that hooked nose and cruel mouth. He noted her blond hair, worn high on her head, and her clothing - a long, black velvet gown; hardly the most practical of choices when walking at the dead of night. However the Lady of Clehy had never been ordinary and Servo knew that she certainly would never blend in.

Her ambitions were far loftier.

'Are you sure that it's him, the Guardian and the Chosen One?' the male voice asked.

The woman replied, 'For certain it is him; and he is with that woman – with Dywana.' She spat out this last word with such venom that even the listener flinched.

From her accent it was clear she wasn't from Cornwall. Servo knew where this woman came from. It was a land far from these shores: a land of tall mountains, deep lakes and dark pine forests. A land where people had a habit of disappearing.

'What of the others?'

'They are gathering,' the woman replied. 'Soon they will all be together.'

The concealed figure drew further back while the conversation continued.

The male voice said, 'Why wait? Why not press our advantage?'

'We have to wait. It has to be at the right hour and in the right place. Besides, Brane wants revenge for the spilt blood.'

'For Matearnas?'

'Of course for Matearnas! However Brane will learn that I make a far better Queen than ever Matearnas would.'

There was silence.

The invisible spectator stood unmoving; he could stay as long as was needed. Glancing up he noted that the mist was beginning to thin. He looked at the couple standing a short distance from him, just a few granite tombstones stood between them.

On one gravestone a carved angel stretched its wings and, raising his stone eyebrows, regarded Servo, but the Watcher merely smiled and shook his head. The angel rearranged himself, emitting a dry scraping as each of the stone feathers settled back into place.

One of the couple, the man, spun around, 'Something moved!'

'There is nothing here except for you and me. Calm yourself,' the woman replied scornfully.

'My ears are keen - there was something.'

The other speaker sighed wearily, 'I was told that you were a man of courage, Hagarawall, not someone who could be frightened by the merest of whispers! But come, it is time to be on our way.'

Hagarawall didn't need any encouragement and hurriedly led the way out of the churchyard and back down the steep, gravelled path to the lane which led to the beach. Neither of them observed a low, black shape detach itself from the shadows and follow, padding silently behind them. Nor did they see their observer step out of his hiding-place and nod at the stone angel. And perhaps it was fortunate that they didn't witness the angel flap its wings just once, before settling back in a slightly different position.

Chapter 3

~ Time smuggler ~

Porth Pyra

'Hiya, are you coming over to the festival?' Tamar asked, pressing the phone to her ear as she watched the crowds laughing and joking in the lane outside.

'Nope, I was going to, but I want to keep an eye on Lightning,' Arthur said. 'I think he'll get better more quickly if I stick around.'

'How's he doing?'

'He's picking up. Dywana's been amazing, she's so good with him.'

'Dywana seems to be good with almost everything,' Tamar said. 'I wouldn't mind having an aunt like that. My lot always seem to be falling out with each other over every little thing. It does my head in!'

Arthur didn't reply. He thought about Tamar and her sister who were often in the middle of a heated argument, usually over nothing. Maybe they were continuing the family tradition.

He tried to think of something diplomatic to say but fortunately their conversation was interrupted by a shout. Tamar opened the window and leant out to see Nick waiting in the street below her.

'I've got to go Arthur, Nick's here. Text us if there's any change in Lightning won't you?'

'Yeah course I will. Have fun.'

As he put the phone down, Arthur realised that he hadn't said anything about who he thought might have injured his dog, but perhaps it was better if he kept that to himself. And he decided that for now he was quite happy to stay at the cottage.

Over in Porth Pyra, Tamar closed the window, jumped off the window seat and, grabbing a pile of clothes, ran down the stairs. She loved this time of year when the village was decked out in all its finery for the annual summer festival. There was always so much going on.

'Hi, come in… and don't look like that!'

'Like what?' Nick asked.

'Like you've never seen a skirt before,' Tamar replied.

'Yeah, but *you* in a skirt, I thought you were born wearing jeans!'

'It's for the festival, everyone's in fancy dress. Or haven't you noticed?'

And at that very moment a group of would-be smugglers passed the cottage door, closely followed by a crowd of pirates wearing eye-patches, a few of them even had toy parrots pinned to their shoulders. Yapping dogs stirred up by the activity all around them, strained on their leads, and excited children tugged at their parents' hands.

See?' Tamar said, grabbing Nick and pulling him into the cottage. Then she pushed a bundle of clothes at him, 'Here you are.'

'What's this for?' he asked.

'For you to wear, of course!'

'This is a girl's blouse, I'm not wearing that!' he said, holding up one of the pieces suspiciously.

'It's not a blouse - it's a floppy shirt. Come on Nick, everyone dresses up. '

'So what am I meant to be?'

'A pirate, it's obvious. Come on, we're going to miss it if you don't hurry.'

He looked at the clothes and at Tamar, standing with her hands on her hips, and knew that this was one battle he wouldn't win.

'Oh, okay,' he agreed, reluctantly.

'Good, I'll wait down here,' she said. 'You go upstairs.'

Tamar pointed to the narrow stairs winding up to the sitting room above them. 'Go on!'

'Never knew you had to dress up,' Nick muttered under his breath, climbing the stairs. But to Tamar he said, 'How's Lightning doing? '

'Arthur says he's doing okay, but he's not coming over 'cause he doesn't want to leave him… and Gawain has to help out in the shop again.'

'Oh,' Nick said, trying to hide his disappointment.

However Tamar wasn't fooled, 'You'll have to put up with me for company today!'

'No, it's just…'

'Just what?' she shouted up the stairs.

'Oh, nothing.' Nick said.

The thing was, he knew that he and Tamar were a bad combination when they were left together for more than five minutes. One or the other of them would say something and before they knew it, there'd be an argument brewing. More often than not it was his fault because he couldn't resist winding her up. Well Arthur wasn't here, so he'd have to try to get through the whole day without teasing her.

He looked at the clothes she was expecting him to change into and decided that, although it was against his natural instincts, he'd humour her.

The room she'd sent him to mirrored the room below. Dark, knotted beams reached across the ceiling and a curved bay window looked out onto the lane. Mug Shot, Tamar's dog, was curled up in a basket in a corner of the room and the moment he saw Nick his tail started to thump out a greeting.

'Hello boy,' Nick said, stroking his head. 'Aren't you allowed out?'

'No he's not,' Tamar shouted up the stairs. 'He gets too excited and then he's a pain.'

'Poor dog,' Nick said to Mug Shot. 'It can't be fun having such a strict owner.'

'Oh, shut up and get changed!' Tamar ordered.

Nick smiled to himself before he remembered his resolution. He'd have to try harder. He pulled the shirt over his head and checked his reflection in the dusty mirror propped up against the wall. His hair, blond and tousled, was a mess but he decided that it added to the piratical theme Tamar seemed so keen on. He sighed as he contemplated the shirt, or blouse. It was probably just as well that the other two weren't coming. They'd die laughing.

A few minutes later they were outside and Nick found himself being swept along by noisy, jostling crowds. They were all heading away from the harbour, through the narrow lanes and towards the village square where most of the activities took place.

Tamar shouted above the noise, 'It'll be loads of fun - they've got some good acts this year.'

Nick didn't reply because he was still getting used to wearing what he was sure was a girl's blouse, despite anything Tamar had said.

On a mossy roof a crow monitored their progress up the street, while behind them a woman kept pace, gliding in and out of the crowds. She was unusually tall, with blond hair piled high on her head, and was wearing a floor-length, black velvet dress. As the woman slipped among the crowds, always a few paces behind Nick and Tamar, she attracted curious stares but appeared to be completely unaware of people's reaction to her, or of how they instinctively drew out of her way. Her focus was solely on the two friends a little way ahead.

The procession of smugglers and pirates rounded a corner leading into the village square. Tamar spotted a space close to the band and, grabbing Nick by the hand, dragged him towards the little stage. Nick was feeling more and more out of place; fancy dress and now it looked like there would be dancing too!

He was just about to protest and make his escape when the band struck up. A base drum resonated through the air, setting a heavy beat closely followed by an accordion, and within minutes the square was a mass of whirling, spinning bodies.

Pirates, male and female, young and old, weaved among smugglers of all shapes and sizes. Toy parrots jiggled on shoulders, children jumped and shrieked while those too old to dance tapped their feet to the heady beat.

Suddenly Tamar found her hand being taken by a man wearing the most convincing of costumes. He looked every inch the smuggler, even down to a pistol tucked into his belt. His moustache was oiled and waxed into place, curling up at the ends, and beneath white eyebrows his dark eyes twinkled.

'Zephaniah Jenner at your service, Ma'am,' he said, bowing with a flourish.

She giggled, 'Tamar ...'

Then Zephaniah took her hand, cast a quick look behind him and Tamar found herself being whirled around as the music picked up speed and grew louder and louder.

'Now Ma'am, we must take great care,' he said as they danced towards a stone arch straddling the lane, 'methinks this is the place.'

Tamar wondered where Nick had got to because there was no sign of him.

'Hang on a minute, wait for my friend.' She wasn't sure that she was happy being guided by this strange man.

But her dancing partner just cast a quick look towards the crowd saying, 'Your friend? No Ma'am, he will be entertained.'

And with that he proceeded to spin Tamar round and round until the world was a dizzy blur of bodies and she was at the edge of the dancers. Another couple of beats from the drum and a chord from a guitar, and they were through the arch and the bright sunlight dimmed. In that instant all the crowds disappeared to be replaced by dark streets, empty of people. Immediately Zephaniah stopped dancing and hastily pulled Tamar away from the arch and towards a row of low stone-built cottages.

'In here Ma'am,' he said urgently, glancing up and down the dark lane. 'Before *she* finds us.'

But Tamar was too stunned to move.

She looked around at the narrow, now-cobbled, lanes and up at the starlit sky. Not only had the day become night, but not a single note of music had followed them.

In the blink of an eye the village had been converted from one filled with lively, laughing people into a silent fishing port. The cottages, which moments before had obviously been carefully renovated and immaculately painted, were now stripped of all their twenty-first century glory. Instead, bare stonework and unpainted wooden doors lined the street, the homes of simple fishing families.

'How…' was all she had time to say before an elegant foot appeared in the archway.

Gripping her hand, Zephaniah ducked his head beneath a wooden lintel and swiftly led Tamar through a low doorway and into a darkened, stone-floored room. He swung the door closed behind them and put a warning finger to his lips, shaking his head as Tamar opened her mouth to protest.

Despite her confusion she did as he said.

It broke all the rules she'd ever been taught about trusting people she didn't know, but something about this man reminded her of Michael Jolly, and she would have trusted him with her life.

Footsteps echoed down the lane, coming closer before coming to a halt outside the door.

Tamar held her breath. She had no idea who, or what, was outside but a clammy chill was spreading through her. Furthermore her sword, which had been warm, was now icy cold.

There was silence; their stalker was sniffing them out.

After what was probably only a couple of minutes, but seemed like an eternity, there was a movement outside the door and then the footsteps were walking away from the cottage and on down the lane. Their hiding place was secure.

For now.

It was a while before either she or Zephaniah moved.

Eventually he whispered, 'T'was a lucky escape, we must make haste.'

He fished out a key from a pocket in his frock coat, 'Forgive me Ma'am,' he said quietly. 'There be no time now for explanations.'

Tamar was struggling with more than merely being chased. Her brain was telling her that it was impossible to walk from day into night, but her senses were sending her a different message.

Zephaniah, watching her, appeared to understand her thoughts.

'There is much to tell but my task is only to be the messenger. I too was appointed a Guardian, as I believe you 'ave been.'

Immediately Tamar was pulled back to the present - wherever that was.

'How did you know that I'm a Guardian?' she asked. 'Were you there? Were you on the moor last summer?'

'No, I was in my own time, Michael told me.'

'Michael! He came to see you?' Tamar said, her head reeling. 'We haven't seen him since last year. Why did he come to see you and not bother coming to see us?'

At this Zephaniah's mouth began to twitch, 'Ah, a woman of fire. I understand now why you were chosen.'

Despite her situation Tamar could feel her temper beginning to flare, but before anything else could be said Zephaniah was striding across the little room. Tamar looked around and noticed that there were no lights or heaters and started to wonder how old the cottage could be, but her attention was drawn back to her host. By now he was kneeling down on the dusty floor and muttering to himself, while unlocking a battered, wooden chest. The only light came from a strip of moonlight forcing its way beneath the wooden shutters, so it was a few moments before he triumphantly pulled a package from its depths.

'I have it!' he said, clutching the object.

'This must be taken to The One appointed as the Guide - The One charged with the care of Cornwall and her people.'

Tamar frowned, trying to work out Zephaniah's meaning. 'Oh! Do you mean Arthur?'

'Arthur,' Zephaniah paused thoughtfully. 'So 'e is named as our King was named.'

'*Your* King?'

'Indeed Ma'am, King Arthur, King of Cornwall,' he said.

'There wasn't a real King Arthur!'

Zephaniah froze as if he'd been struck, before gathering himself and saying quietly, 'Ma'am, 'ow can you say such a thing!'

Even though a part of her brain was telling her to be quiet, her mouth was taking no notice - as usual.

'He's a myth, or a legend isn't he? I'm sure one of our teachers told us that he'd never existed.'

Yet even as she was saying this, Tamar's thoughts were with that history teacher who'd appeared just over a year ago and, just as mysteriously, disappeared. The teacher had seemed old, with her hair twisted into a tight, grey bun, but she'd had the air of someone much younger. Then Tamar remembered a conversation they'd had about mythical heroes. Although the teacher hadn't said as much, she'd implied that some legendary figures posed a difficulty for other history teachers. Many of them preferred to explain them away. It was easier than having to believe in them.

There was silence. Zephaniah looked as if he'd been cut through by her words and he sighed so deeply that Tamar wished she could take back everything she'd said.

'I'm sorry - it's only what we've been told.'

'Ma'am, the fault is not yours, but that of others. You are young.'

He paused, considering his words, 'Suffice it to say that your elders do not always 'ave true knowledge.'

Tamar was on the point of asking Zephaniah how he was so certain that King Arthur had existed, when she caught herself. She'd been whisked from day to night and maybe also to another time - although her mind danced away from this possibility. What was real? She closed her mouth before she could say something else she might regret. Perhaps there was more to the legend than she'd been taught. Maybe that history teacher had had a point.

Zephaniah was watching her. It was almost as if he was reading Tamar's thoughts because he smiled very slightly, nodded and held out the package.

'I would wish to talk more on this matter but there is little time. You must return before we are found. Give this to The One appointed as Guardian an' Guide of Kernow. It must be placed in 'is hand.'

Tamar took the package; it was a rolled piece of parchment, tied with ribbon. The sword around her neck had changed from icy-cold to warm. She wondered if it was glowing.

'You are entrusted above many others, Ma'am. Now come.'

He pulled the door open. Tamar heard footsteps coming closer.

'Quickly Ma'am!'

And she was being thrust through the archway, from the moonlight to sunlight, and from an empty lane into a teeming street.

A tiny crackle, a '*woomph*' and two shadows followed her out of the archway. One of them was a walker, complete with a backpack and a woolly hat, and the other was a fisherman (wearing rather odd shoes).

'The gift has been given.'

Servo, the walker, replied, 'Yes, Zephaniah has played his part well. Now it is for the girl to fulfil her assignment.'

Viatoris nodded and added, 'The Writer is here too.'

The other Watcher looked at him sharply, 'Where? I haven't seen her!'

His companion tried not to look smug, but again he didn't succeed. 'The Writer has been here in Porth Pyra and at Porth Talant. I believe she will call you soon'.

Servo looked offended, 'Why has she called you and not me?'

Both the Watchers were assigned to the Writer, a woman of influence. A woman who supervised the comings and goings of her time-travelling team and their charges. Her appearance was rather like an old-fashioned head-teacher, complete with grey hair in a tight bun and glasses worn on a string around her neck, but any similarity ended there. Head Teachers don't generally travel through time.

'Maybe you were too far off to call. Maybe you were occupied Watching Joseph in Egypt. It is many years away, is it not?' Viatoris continued with hardly a pause, smoothly discussing Tamar. 'The girl was not alone when she journeyed across the years. She was followed through the Gate.'

'Yes,' Servo replied curtly. 'I saw her follower too.'

He was still smarting from the implied criticism of his late arrival – and that the other Watcher had already met the Writer - when a movement in the archway alerted him and he stepped back into the shadows just as an elegant foot appeared, swept by a floor-length velvet skirt.

Chapter 4

~ Dragon ~

Tamar looked up at the blue, summer sky and back to the arch, but there was no clue to suggest that it was also a gateway to another time. And then a raft of memories came flooding back: of dancing angels in a grandfather clock, a cat which could change from ginger to black and, of course, the sword. Just like last summer, her reality was shifting.

Suddenly she remembered the footsteps they'd heard advancing as she'd been plunged back into her world. There was someone following her but she had no idea who, or what, it was.

She scanned the crowd, anxiously searching for Nick, it was vital that they escaped before her mysterious follower caught up with them.

Then she spotted him. He was being spun in tight circles by an enthusiastic, and slightly bossy, female pirate. If Tamar hadn't been so anxious to escape she might have enjoyed the look of pain written across his face, it was obvious that he was having the worst time of his life.

She pushed through the swirling crowds, past the men, women and children who were oblivious to the drama that had taken place just meters away and only minutes before. Past people unaware of a sinister shadow lurking the other side of the arch in another time, but in a similar place. However Tamar was only too aware of her unknown pursuer and, avoiding the dancers' stamping feet and pointed elbows, pressed on until she reached Nick.

Grasping his sleeve, Tamar shouted over the music, 'Nick, we've got to go!'

The female pirate protested, 'He can't go, he's dancing with me!'

However Nick, recognising an escape route when he saw one, made some rather insincere apologies while detaching himself from his partner's clutches, and followed Tamar. It was possibly the one and only time he'd been so keen to do something that she'd suggested.

'What's up?' he asked.

'We've got to get away.'

'But you were desperate to get here!'

'I'll tell you about it later,' she replied, looking over her shoulder for her unknown adversary.

Something told her not to run or to draw undue attention towards herself, but to try to melt into the crowds. She turned and started walking away from the square, weaving in and out of the dancers.

Nick caught up with her, 'What's happened?'

'We've got to get to Arthur - I've been given something I've got to give him. Look, I'll explain later,' she said, pushing the packet deep into her skirt pocket.

She looked around. Perched on a chimney was a large, black-feathered bird.

'It's back, Nick,' she whispered.

'What's back?'

'Look up there.'

And Nick, following her gaze, understood. Watching their every move was a crow. It might not be the same one but, if it was, Nick knew that it was imperative to find a place where they'd be hidden from the bird's sight. If the crow was close so was his master, the Crow Man. He looked up and down the lane, he couldn't see another way out, but then he glanced at a sign swinging from the wall above him and realised that they were right beside the open door of an ancient pub, 'The Three Smugglers'.

'Quick! In here,' he said, tugging Tamar towards the doorway.

For a few moments they paused in the wooden porch while adjusting to the dim light and the noise. Blackened beams, bent and cracked with age, supported the low, sagging ceiling. The furnishings consisted of dark wooden tables and benches coated in layers of varnish, which had probably been unchanged for decades. The result was a feeling of the past reaching out through the warm shadows of the present, a feeling of continuity. Fishermen and smugglers had probably been drinking here for centuries and just for a split-second Tamar was distracted, pondering on how old this place really was, before a distant 'caw' pulled her back to the present. Tamar checked the room, searching for a familiar face or someone who might help them, before realising that one of her sister's friends was working behind the bar.

'Come on,' she said to Nick, 'I know the barmaid. She might be able to help us.'

She forced her way through the would-be pirates and smugglers until she was in front of the high, wooden bar. Voices boomed off the ceiling and walls, and laughter punctuated the conversations all around them.

'Becky?' she said.

The barmaid handed a brimming glass to a tattooed pirate before turning to Tamar.

'What are you doin' in here, Tamar?' she asked, leaning on the bar. 'Morwenna would be mad if she knew that you were in a pub! 'Sides, I thought you'd be up at the Square.'

'We were, but... look can we go through to the garden?'

The barmaid looked closely at Tamar, 'Are you in trouble?'

'Sort of... I think there's someone following us.'

'Someone following you, who is it?' Becky looked around as if she might spot Tamar's stalker. 'You show me and I'll sort them out!'

Looking at Becky, Tamar had no doubt that if it was a normal person who was following them she'd easily 'sort them out'; but she knew that whoever was after them would be far from normal and a challenge, even for Becky. By now Nick had joined in and was asking if there was another way out of the pub and Becky was pointing to a door at the back of the crowded bar.

'You can go out that way if you like,' she looked worried. 'Why don't you stay here? It'd be safer.'

Tamar shook her head. She would have loved to stay in the pub, enfolded in its warm welcome and muffled against danger, but she'd been charged with getting this package to Arthur.

'No thanks Becky, but maybe you could stop anyone else from going out of the pub through that door? For a while anyway.'

The barmaid was about to protest again and to persuade them to stay with her, but Nick and Tamar were already making their way to the back of the packed room, forcing their way through the forest of elbows and raised glasses, towards the door leading to the garden. Becky watched them for a moment, undecided as to what to do, before shaking her head and starting to organise a group of fishermen leaning up against the bar.

'Boys,' she said, 'would you let these two through and then lock the garden door behind them?'

Instantly the men stopped talking and moved aside to let Tamar and Nick through, but it was one man in particular who took control. This man was tall and bearded, with powerful arms and broad shoulders and, although they were preoccupied with evading their hunter, they both noted the tattoos of mermaids, dolphins and seals swimming along his arms as he pointed to a path winding through the garden.

'Follow that to the end,' he said. 'There be a gate at the top. It'll take you through to the cliff way.'

Their helper paused before adding under his breath so only they could hear, 'We all be 'ere. You tell the Sire, we be ready. *Comero weeth* – take care.'

And before either of them had time to question him, he was closing and locking the door behind them. A second later a stranger ducked through the low doorway of the pub and looked around. Silence fell, unbroken by a clink of a glass or a cough, and the men drew together, barring the way to the garden.

Nick and Tamar ran up the path and through the gate to the cliff walk that would take them to Porth Talant. A large ginger and white cat sat on the wall watching their progress. When they'd disappeared around the bend he meowed once, before making his way purposefully back down the path.

. . .

'Gawain for you,' Dywana said, holding the phone out to Arthur.

'Hiya, are you able to come over?' Arthur asked, as he took the phone. 'It's a bit quiet here. Everyone's gone to Porth Pyra for the festival.'

'Yeah, Pendrym's quiet too,' Gawain answered, 'we've hardly had a customer through the door.' Then he paused and his tone changed. 'Is everything okay at Dywana's? I mean… has anything odd happened?'

'What, apart from Lightning getting hurt?' Arthur asked.

'Yeah, has there been anything else weird?'

'No, apart from the sea mist last night,' Arthur said, thinking about how fast it had rolled in.

'Oh, good,' Gawain said. His relief was obvious.

'Why?'

'Just a feeling. Hey, how about if I walk over to your place? I should be with you in about an hour. Uncle Kitto says I can have the rest of the day off.'

'Yeah, that'd be cool!'

Arthur put the phone down and wondered what could be worrying Gawain. Lightning was still a bit under the weather but he was definitely recovering, so it couldn't be that.

He called out to Dywana, 'Can you keep an eye on the dog? I'm going down to the beach.' He needed time to think.

Arthur cast a hasty eye over the beach and the cliffs for any sign of the Crow Man, or his bird, before pulling the door closed behind him. Seagulls screeched and a blackbird was hard at work in Dywana's garden, intent on finding worms or beetles, but no dark shape cawed raucously to his master. He breathed out and vaguely noted that the cat was still not back from its wanderings.

The sea was glassy calm and the little bay was quiet, not one other person was there. He supposed that the festival at Porth Pyra had lured the holiday-makers away from the beach but it felt good to have it all to himself. He was certain that something was about to happen because he had that familiar sense of unease, just like the day last summer when they'd so narrowly escaped from the Crow Man and ended up at Michael and Angela's house.

Arthur wandered down to the sea and picked up a flat, grey stone. He flicked it expertly, skimming it across the water's surface, when a movement at the edge of the rocks caught his eye as a sleek shape dived into the sea. Fascinated, he started to slip his way over the seaweed to get a closer look. He stood on the edge of the rocks and stared out to sea but, if there had been anything there, it had gone.

Arthur was about to turn away when the atmosphere started to shimmer and ripple, exactly as it had on that magical night a year ago when he'd been shown the knighting of that other Arthur, the legendary King of Cornwall. However, this time nothing so charming was about to take place, because the morning light was dimming and storm clouds were rolling in, blotting out the bright sun.

He looked behind him to the steep land rising up from the beach and saw that the trees were no longer the vivid summer green he'd seen moments before but had been transformed to leafless, winter trees; while the fields had shed their crops in exchange for bare soil. And now, instead of calm water, the sea was boiling and angry, sending huge waves to break over his head – and it was then that he heard the voices.

They were the voices of people pleading for their lives, drowning beneath the waves.

As the wind increased the cries became louder and more desperate, joining together in a frantic chorus. Arthur could hear individuals - men, women and children - and he could hear their words, but he was unable to move, frozen by the horror of what he heard.

But then, as suddenly as it had started the storm ceased and the cries faded; the wind dropped and the clouds rolled away leaving Arthur in a sunlit, summer's day. Except now he was soaked to the skin - with despairing voices echoing in his head.

. . .

'Isn't there an easier way to get to Art's?' Nick asked, puffing, as Tamar led the way up a rocky path carved deep into the side of the cliff.

'No, apart from going miles around on the road.'

'How much further is it?' he asked, looking above him, checking that the sky was clear.

'You've done this walk before, haven't you?' she asked.

'Ages ago, I can't remember.'

'Well,' she said, looking over her shoulder, 'it's not far and it's the best way to get there. You'll just have to trust me.'

As they entered a green tunnel of trees Tamar slowed down to allow them to catch their breath. They were pretty well hidden here.

'So, who was following us back there?' Nick asked. 'I didn't get a chance to see. Was it the Crow Man?'

'Dunno,' she said.

Nick stood stock-still. 'What d'you mean, you don't know?'

'I don't know who's following us,' she said, as if it was perfectly reasonable.

He looked at her dumbfounded.

She shrugged, 'Look, all I know for certain is that someone was after us. You saw the crow didn't you?'

'Yeah, but that's crazy, surely you saw him.'

She considered his question and thought about the footsteps and that elegant toe, 'I don't know if it's just one person, it could be the Crow Man or it could be someone else. It could be a woman... I didn't get a chance to see.'

'Brilliant,' Nick said. 'We're on the run and we don't know who's after us.'

'It's not my fault!'

'Maybe not, but don't take up working as a spy, 'cause it kind of helps to know who's after you.'

Tamar was about to come back with a cutting answer when a rustle in the low branches above them distracted her, and a robin fluttered past Nick's face before landing at his feet. They watched as it started to peck at the earth, drawing their attention to something glinting at the edge of the path. The robin hopped over and started to worry at a small mound of leaves.

Nick knelt down to get a better look. Strangely the robin didn't take fright and fly away but perched above him on a slim branch, monitoring his every move.

'What is it?' Tamar asked.

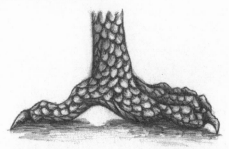

However Nick didn't say a word, he just held up the object. It was a tiny, green-stone dragon. The sculpture was perfect, with every scale on its body and every vein in its wings, sharply defined. Nick marvelled at the workmanship, whoever had carved it must have been a master of their art, it was so uncannily real. He examined it, turning it over and looking at it from every angle, and wondered if it was a trick of the light or whether a claw really had moved.

(Of course it could have been something purely mechanical that caused the dragon's claw to uncurl, stretch and retract but it's unlikely - although most adults might try to believe that that was the reason. After all it would be much easier than explaining something so clearly impossible.)

Chapter 5

~ The Crow Man ~

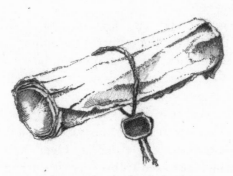

Gawain sat on the rug in Arthur's bedroom, stroking Lightning and watching the model sailing ship on Arthur's window sill because, from time to time, its sails would fill and the ship would rock as if it was at sea.

'Who gave you the ship?' Gawain asked, nodding towards the model.

'I'm not sure, it's been here forever,' Arthur replied. 'It could have been Great-Uncle Lance... but I can't remember.'

'Has it always done that?' Gawain asked, as the ship swayed in the imaginary wind.

'No, I don't think so. I've a feeling that's quite recent, probably since last summer. It's cool though, isn't it?'

'Yeah, in a weird sort of way,' Gawain agreed.

'Hey, remember where my other stone knight came from! How many other shops do you know which sell stone models that change temperature?'

Gawain pretended to give the question serious thought, 'You mean it's not just ours?'

Arthur threw his wet t-shirt at him. It was reassuring to have company after what had happened that morning.

'Anyway,' he said, pulling on a dry shirt, 'what's bothering you?'

'I'm not exactly sure,' Gawain replied. 'It's just that there's a strange feeling around Pendrym. You know that feeling when the atmosphere's heavy and there's going to be a massive thunderstorm? Well, it sort of feels like that... all the time.'

Arthur cast his mind back to the previous summer and Gawain's part in his rescue. He didn't question Gawain's intuition for a minute. Over the past twelve months he'd got used to his friend's uncanny ability to know when something unusual was going to happen. 'Is it like when you tried to stop me going into the Granite House? You knew there was something about to happen then didn't you?'

Gawain leant back against the wall thinking about Arthur's capture by the Crow Man and Matearnas.

'Yeah, in a way it's the same, but that time I had a much clearer idea. This time it's more of a general threat and... '

Gawain trailed off, trying to find the right words.

'And what?'

'Well, this is going to sound a bit crazy,' Gawain said.

'Go on,' Arthur replied, thinking nothing could match the craziness of that morning on the beach.

'I think it has something to do with stuff that happened ages ago.'

'What sort of stuff?' Arthur asked.

'I don't know - I wish I did,' Gawain said. 'It's as if there's someone calling out to me but I can't hear the words.'

There was silence, broken only by Lightning's snores and the ship's creaks as it lurched from side to side.

Throwing a pile of clothes onto the floor, Arthur settled into an old armchair squeezed between the bed and the wall. He knew that he shouldn't keep what had happened to himself.

'Something strange happened to me this morning,' he said.

Gawain stopped stroking Lightning.

'It was really bizarre,' Arthur added.

'So, it's not just me then,' Gawain said.

'No, though I wish it was! Look, this is going to sound stupid.'

He took a deep breath. 'I was down on the beach. There was nobody else around; it was completely deserted so I thought that everybody must have gone to the festival but now I'm not so sure ...'

'And?'

'Well, I thought I saw a seal, so I climbed out to the furthest rocks ...'

'What happened - did you fall in?' Gawain asked.

Arthur shook his head, '*That* would have been okay. No, you know how sunny it's been?'

Gawain nodded.

'Well it was like that, clear blue sky, when this huge storm just came out of nowhere - it was like someone had flicked a switch.'

He paused as he tried to gather the right words to properly describe what had happened.

'It was much more than an ordinary storm because the waves were massive, giant waves, but it wasn't just the sea...' Arthur glanced at Gawain as he added, 'There were voices too, and they weren't ordinary voices having a conversation, they were screaming and crying out, it was really horrible.'

Gawain looked at him, never for a moment doubting what Arthur had described, 'Mate, that's freaky!'

Arthur shuddered, 'It's not something you'd forget in a hurry.'

Gawain was about to speak when an urgent hammering filled the cottage. Lightning sat up, ears pricked, the first time he'd been so alert since he'd been hurt. They heard footsteps cross the hallway and Dywana's voice joined by others, then feet pounding up the stairs and the door was flung open.

'Oh good, you're both here!' Tamar said breathlessly, as she burst into the room.

Nick was just a couple of paces behind her, he poked his head around the door but didn't follow Tamar right in.

'Hi guys,' he said, as he hung back.

'Hiya, come in,' Arthur said.

'It's okay, I'll stay here,' Nick replied, a little awkwardly.

'Oh, come in,' Tamar said impatiently. 'No one cares about what you're wearing!'

'I care,' he mumbled.

Tamar rolled her eyes and, ignoring him, turned to Arthur, 'Is it safe? Is there anyone else here?'

The ship on the windowsill was heaving from side to side, its sails billowing. As Arthur was about to answer there was a meow and the cat strode into the room with its tail held high. It stalked over to Lightning's basket and the dog immediately settled down, then it leapt onto the windowsill, giving the ship a wide berth, and sat surveying the activity on the, now busy, beach.

'It's the same cat isn't it?' Nick said to no one in particular and reluctantly edged in to join his friends. But he needn't have worried about their reaction because both Arthur and Gawain's attention had been drawn to Tamar - something was obviously worrying her. Even though they were safely in the cottage she was quite clearly on edge.

They watched her as she shut the door and checked the window, ensuring that what she was about to say wouldn't be overheard and that no one other than her fellow Guardians would see the package she'd been given for Arthur.

Arthur looked at her curiously, 'What's up?'

'I've been given something for you. I was told that I had to make sure it reached you.'

By now she had their complete attention. 'And I think someone else wants it too.'

'Who?' Gawain asked.

'I don't know.'

'What!' Arthur exclaimed.

Tamar sighed, 'All I know is that we were being followed.'

'Well, she *thinks* we were,' Nick interrupted. 'I couldn't see anybody.'

'Oh come on Nick, you saw the bird too!' Tamar said, spinning around to face him.

'Yeah, but I didn't see anyone coming after us,' he said. 'It wasn't like it was with the Crow Man; maybe it was an ordinary crow. Perhaps it was the crowds or something that spooked you.' As he said this he felt a sharp stab in his hand and remembered the stone dragon.

He opened his pocket and peered in. Had the tail moved?

Tamar began to protest but remembered the urgency with which Zephaniah had spoken - and what he'd asked her to do. She couldn't waste time arguing with Nick.

'Oh, forget it!' she said. 'It doesn't matter.'

And with that she pulled the scroll out of her skirt pocket.

A hush settled over the room as she handed the packet to Arthur. The ribbon tying it had faded since Tamar had been given it that morning, and the parchment had already yellowed and curled at the edges. In the space of just an hour or so, the scroll had aged by many years, possibly even by centuries. And immediately each one of them had their chains in their hands because the swords were now warm as if they had recognised an ally - and the cat had begun to purr.

Arthur's hands shook as he untied the ribbon. 'Who gave this to you?'

'An old guy, um probably very old,' Tamar said thoughtfully as she considered Zephaniah and the unlit, stone-floored cottage. Could she really have travelled to another time? It didn't bear thinking about, life was already quite complicated enough! She shook her head, as if that might help to dismiss the thoughts of her encounter, and added, 'He was very insistent.'

'How did he know about me?' Arthur asked.

'I don't know, but he called you 'Sire'. Oh! And he was a Guardian, like us.'

'You didn't tell me any of that,' Nick protested.

'I know but there wasn't time... and I didn't want to talk about it until we were somewhere safe. Perhaps next time you'll believe me if I say we're being followed!'

'It might have helped if you'd told me about the old guy!' Nick retorted.

There was an awkward silence.

'Go on then, open it!' Nick said to Arthur, turning his back on Tamar.

Arthur glanced from one to the other. As far as he was concerned, now wasn't the time for arguments. Tamar bit her lip, picking up on Arthur's impatience, and swallowed all the replies that were coming to mind. Instead she said, 'Yeah, go on; let's see what's in there.'

There was a collective silence as Arthur pulled at the ribbon and the scroll uncoiled. In the centre was a sort of faded map or picture, but its location was unclear. Underneath the map writing meandered across the bottom edge of the parchment, but it was so elaborate and written in such an ancient hand that it was almost impossible to read. However in one corner there was another drawing - and that was very clear.

'It's the same one, isn't it?' Nick remarked.

Arthur nodded. The drawing was of the hilt of the sword he'd held so briefly on that moorland hilltop a year ago.

'Ah,' Tamar said, 'so *that's* why Zephaniah said you had to have it.'

'What does it say?' Nick asked, pointedly ignoring Tamar.

Arthur peered closely at the writing on the yellowed parchment, 'I can't make out the writing, but it looks like it's some sort of verse.'

He looked at Tamar, 'Did this Zephy guy say what it's for?'

She shook her head, 'No, there wasn't time – like I said, we were being followed!'

Suddenly the cat leapt off the windowsill and crossed the room. It scratched at the door, desperate to get outside, as a black shape flew past the window. Catching the movement, Gawain looked out to see purple-black clouds spreading across the sky.

He stood up and craned his neck to get a good look at the beach. The holiday-makers who'd arrived since the morning were hurriedly packing up, rolling their towels into tight bundles and gathering brightly coloured buckets and spades, while casting glances at the threatening sky. The water churned as the wind whipped it up and, further out to sea, yachts struggled against the sudden worsening weather.

'Art,' he said, 'have you got somewhere safe to keep that?'

Reluctantly, Arthur tore himself away from examining the words inscribed on the scroll, and both Nick and Tamar looked out of the window.

The last of the families were scurrying towards the top of the beach, urging their children to hurry as the sky darkened and the first fat drops of rain began to fall. Car doors were slamming and the beach car park was rapidly emptying, leaving the sandy bay space to recover from being trampled and explored.

Except the beach wasn't entirely deserted because now, standing in splendid isolation and undisturbed by the wind and the rain, was the solitary Crow Man. He glanced around, checking for any lingering tourists, and then slowly turned towards them and lifted his arms to the skies. A flash of lightning burnt across the bay and the Crow Man tilted his head back and lifted his arms higher. They watched, transfixed, as the wind gathered strength and the thunder boomed, conducted by a man in a broad-brimmed hat with a bird by his side.

He had their complete attention - and he knew it. He stared up at the window while his wild orchestra played, and he grinned. And Arthur was back in Station Road in Lyskeret, re-living their first nightmare meeting when his world had been changed forever.

'So, he *is* back again!' Arthur muttered, clutching the scroll. 'And he knows where we are.'

His friends turned from watching their enemy and regarded Arthur. For several minutes no-one said a word because they all knew that if the Crow Man was involved no-one, and nothing, was safe. But by the time they looked out of the window again the beach was empty.

Their adversary had disappeared.

Chapter 6

~ A touch of ice ~

Dywana was calling to them from the hallway.

'Tamar, your sister's been lookin' for you. Jago's here and he said that he can take you and Nick back to Porth Pyra.'

No one answered her.

Instead Tamar asked Arthur, 'What's going to happen; now *he's* back?'

He shrugged despondently, 'I've no idea.' The reappearance of his adversary had finally dashed all of his hopes that Porth Talant was a safe haven.

They looked out of the window at the abandoned beach as the ship on the windowsill veered wildly from side to side, rocked by its own invisible storm. Then Nick suddenly leant forward and pointed to the wall running along the top of the sandy bay.

'Look!'

Cats - there must have been close to a hundred of them in all shapes, sizes and colours.

Some were sitting, others were washing and one or two were looking out to sea, but most intriguing was that 'their' cat was sauntering along the base of the wall as if he was inspecting his troops. As he reached each animal it would stand to attention, then leap off the wall and casually make its way up the lane.

'It's just like before!' Tamar exclaimed.

Gawain looked puzzled and then his face cleared, 'Oh, is this what happened in Lyskeret?'

'Yeah, exactly the same,' Arthur said, as he looked out of the window. 'Our very own private army – except that it's made up of a bunch of cats!'

Then he turned from looking out of the window and eyed Nick and Tamar, 'Look, you two had better be going.'

'But there's more I've got to tell you,' Tamar protested.

'Yeah, but if Dywana thinks it's time for you guys to go, you've got to go, she'll have her reasons - you can text me when you're back.'

His face was set and both Nick and Tamar recognised that he'd made his mind up.

'Okay,' Tamar finally agreed, 'if you think so. We'll see you tomorrow at Pendrym.'

Arthur nodded and followed his friends to the top of the stairs to see both Dywana, and the fisherman who'd rescued Lightning, waiting for them. His aunt was fidgeting and already had her hand on the front door catch.

This was not the calm Dywana he'd come to know.

He watched and listened as the front door scraped open, and Tamar and Nick were ushered into the garden, while Dywana said to Jago, '*Comero weeth*!'

'Don't worry,' he heard Jago reply, 'they'll be safe enough.'

And then he heard the added comment, 'T'is for Kernow.'

However he didn't see her nod, her face grim, as she replied, 'I know Jago.'

Arthur returned to his room and, with Gawain, watched their friends as they followed Jago down the beach past the few remaining cats and clambered into the waiting boat, all the time studiously ignoring one another.

As he climbed into the boat, Nick looked back to the cottage perched at the top of the beach between the sand and the soil, and waved to Arthur and Gawain. Then he remembered the carved dragon stowed safely in his pocket, he'd meant to show it to Arthur but with the re-appearance of the Crow Man he'd completely forgotten about it.

Meanwhile Tamar was studying the hills behind the cottage. There was no sign of any movement among the trees but they grew so close together it would have been difficult to spot anybody. Especially someone who didn't want to be seen - and the Watcher was determined to remain invisible for now.

The boat glided, creaking, out of the little bay and towards the open sea. Jago rowed mechanically while inspecting the woods and fields rising up behind the beach. A shadow moved between the trees and at first Jago tensed and scanned the skies for a dark bird but then he relaxed as he caught sight of a woolly hat. The Watcher, observing them from the tree-cloaked hillside, might be well hidden from ordinary eyes but Jago's eyes or life could hardly be classed as conventional. The unusually-gifted fisherman smiled to himself as he recognised the hat. It was the stripy knitted one worn by one of the Watchers and thankfully not the broad-brimmed hat favoured by the Crow Man.

Reassured that the Guardians' enemy wasn't too close by, Jago glanced down to the clear waters and remarked, '*Morahas.*'

'*Morahas?*' Tamar repeated, mystified.

'Dolphins.'

Tamar had been enthralled by dolphins for as long as she could remember. She'd read about them, watched programmes about them and even had a couple of posters on her bedroom wall. However she'd never, until now, seen them in the wild.

Jago nodded towards the water, 'Look.'

Tamar followed his gaze and saw that, sure enough, a pod of dark, silky bodies were twisting and weaving through the water beside them.

'Oh....' she whispered, 'they're so beautiful!'

'They be 'ere to see you safely home,' Jago said.

Tamar looked at him doubtfully just as a dolphin leapt clean out of the water, showering them with salty spray, and Jago chuckled, 'Now, that's just a bit of showin' off.'

'Wow, that's amazing!' Nick said, leaning over to catch a better view.

'T'is a rare honour,' the fisherman stated.

He started to row back down the coast towards Porth Pyra, skirting the razor-like rocks hidden beneath the surface. The dolphins swam around the tiny craft, almost touching Tamar and Nick's outstretched hands.

Jago looked from the creatures to his passengers, and smiled quietly to himself. He'd noticed their initial awkwardness with one another and now he watched it melt away under the magical influence of their escorts, it worked every time. He rowed, satisfied that his passengers' argument would soon be forgotten, and turned to studying the girl. As soon as he'd set eyes on her he'd seen the faint light which encircled her, it was almost oozing out of her pores. If he'd been asked to describe it he would have struggled, but the most accurate description would have been sepia shot through with flecks of gold. Jago reflected on the other instances when he'd encountered this particular phenomenon and knew that it could only mean one thing. Tamar Tamblyn had been time-travelling. He continued to row – and speculated on where she'd been.

As the boat entered Porth Pyra's harbour the dolphins swam away, their duty was done, and Nick and Tamar grinned at each other. Not only was their argument forgotten but the dolphins' presence had also banished the darkness spread by the Crow Man's reappearance. It was as if the creatures had absorbed all the strange and unusual events of the day.

'That was brilliant,' Nick said, leaning over the side to watch their escorts disappear. 'I've never seen them so close. Perhaps they came nearer because it's a small boat.'

'Perhaps,' Jago said, smiling.

However Tamar had already turned her attention back to the village, wondering who might be waiting there, but the only person she could see that she knew was her sister standing on the edge of the harbour wall. She wasn't able to pick out those others who were watching from the jumble of cottages crowding the valley floor.

...

The Writer sat outside a café in Porth Pyra and watched the little boat as it approached the quayside. Jago Jolliff could always be relied upon and, although he wasn't within her jurisdiction, it was satisfying to see a job done well. He'd ensured the safe return of Nick and Tamar but, watching Tamar's sister, the Writer doubted that Morwenna would see it that way.

Then she saw the light, invisible to most, surrounding Tamar; so the girl must have been time-travelling. The Writer smiled, pleased that she'd been proved to be right. This girl was not only destined to be a Guardian but also a Time Traveller. The Writer watched and listened, knowing it would soon be time to Write.

...

Tamar saw her sister spot them and start to run towards the landing jetty.

'Oh no, I'm going to be in *so* much trouble.'

Nick, looking at Morwenna, silently agreed and wished he could quietly disappear. Tamar's sister was formidable when she was in a good mood, but looking at her now she looked like she was ready to take on the Crow Man. She stood with her hands on her hips, a larger version of Tamar, with her black hair hanging straight to her waist and her brown eyes flashing.

'What do you think you've been doing?' Morwenna started as soon as they landed. 'I've nearly been out of my mind. Becky told me that some weird person was after you – and I couldn't find you anywhere. You didn't even have your phone switched on!'

Tamar was climbing out of the boat but as she did so she managed to pull her phone out of her pocket. Silently, she handed it to her sister. Morwenna glanced at it and, seeing that it was switched on, calmed down a little. Nick was impressed that Tamar did this without even saying a word. She was obviously used to having to deal with her sister.

He turned to the fisherman, 'Think Morwenna's a bit worked up!'

Jago chuckled, 'T'is an awesome sight, them Tamblyn women, when they be angry. T'is best to keep out of their way.'

The fisherman smiled, 'Around here we call them Tamblyn girls the Daughters of Taran – the Daughters of Thunder.'

Nick contemplated Tamar and her more fiery moments, and decided that Jago was a man of extreme wisdom, although there was no way he'd dare tell Tamar or Wenna!

'Thanks for the um, lift, or whatever,' Nick said.

'T'is an honour. I be glad to help.'

Then Jago added, *'Na rewh nakevy - comero weeth.'*

'Pardon?'

"Don't forget - take care' - t'is the old words,' the man explained, pushing the boat off before heading back out of the harbour.

Nick watched him pull the boat through the water and thought about the words, and about Jago's ability to appear just when he was required. And that phrase, *'Comero weeth'*, he'd heard it quite often recently. *'Comero weeth'* - take care.

Thoughtfully, he turned away from watching Jago's boat slip out of the harbour and followed Morwenna and Tamar, the Daughters of Taran, up the lane towards the cottage. Morwenna was still lecturing her sister but, from behind them, Nick couldn't make out what sort of defence Tamar was putting up.

He was contemplating all that had happened during the day, and wondering how long he'd have to wait for a bus back to town, when he caught sight of a woman dressed in floor-length black velvet, leaning into a wall. She was unusually tall, emphasised by her hair being piled high on her head, and her nose was large and hooked. Nick thought that if she was a bird she'd probably be an eagle. But what particularly caught his eye was her concentration, and that her subject was Tamar. She had her head tilted at an angle and her claw-like fingers twitched as if she was about to take flight and come swooping down on her prey for the kill. Nick hung back and watched. Yet as he looked, it was as if she became aware that she was being scrutinised because, very slowly, she swivelled to face him.

And now it was Nick who was being studied. The woman focused on him and in that instant his world changed, and instead of being in a sleepy, Cornish fishing village he was lost in a dark, pine forest. Tall trees stretched out on every side, reaching up to the sky and blotting out any light. Nick could even smell the musty earth beneath his feet and knew that he was hopelessly alone. Fingers of frost began spreading out, snaking over the ground, creeping up every blade of grass and along every branch and twig, until his world was white and frozen. The cold began to slither and slip into his bones, and he was suddenly overwhelmed by a dark despair sucking any glimmer of hope out of his soul.

The woman smiled; she knew just what he was seeing and feeling. She gazed at him with wide, unblinking eyes, with her head on one side, just as a hawk might survey a mouse, while a slight smile pulled at her lips as she observed her work and its effect upon her victim. By now Nick was shivering, his teeth were chattering and he could feel the beginning of chilblains throbbing in his toes and fingers. She waited a moment more until, finally, content that she had demonstrated her power, the woman turned away and the images immediately disappeared, returning Nick to the world he knew. The woman was no longer interested in him. She'd made her point. And flicking one last, brief glance at Tamar she disappeared down a side alley.

But she left Nick shaking, while the sword around his neck was winter-cold. He didn't trust himself to move. How could she have done that? He waited, allowing his pulse to slow down and the shivering to subside, before he was ready to follow Tamar and Morwenna. He didn't want Tamar to see the after-effects of his encounter.

Slowly, his legs still shaking, he approached the entrance to the little alley and peered around the corner, but there was no sign of the woman. Nick breathed out a frosty breath, and looked up and down the street, checking that she really had gone, before he stamped his feet and rubbed his hands together in an effort to restore his circulation while he thought. Any immediate threat seemed to have passed but he had to warn Tamar about the woman straightaway. It was vital that he told her about what she'd done to him. But he wasn't given an opportunity.

'The next bus is due in about ten minutes, Nick,' Morwenna said, as he caught up with them at the cottage. 'If you hurry you should catch it.'

'But... I..' he started, desperate to talk to Tamar.

'Have you got everything?'

He caught Tamar's eye but she just shrugged; she knew what her sister was like when she had her mind made up.

Nick positioned himself with his back to Morwenna and whispered, 'I saw someone watching you. I think I know who was following you.' He considered trying to tell Tamar just what the woman had done to him, but with Morwenna around it was impossible.

'Don't worry,' Tamar said quietly. 'I've given the scroll to Art. I don't have anything else that anyone would be after - and they'd have to get past Wenna first!'

They were both aware of Tamar's sister pointedly looking at her watch.

'I'm not sure. Listen, will you promise me that you won't go *anywhere* by yourself?' he said seriously.

'What! Are you my brother or something?' Tamar replied, trying to lighten the situation. However it was all too obvious that something had really spooked him. This was a side of Nick she'd never seen before.

'Just promise me you'll be careful... okay?' he urged her; the memory of that bleak despair still lingering and his fingers still numb from the cold.

'Yeah... alright,' Tamar said, momentarily thrown by Nick's obvious concern. But then she recovered herself and added, 'I'll adopt you as my brother if you like, and then I'll have *two* people fussing around me! Look, give me a call and tell me what you saw when you get home.'

However Morwenna was becoming impatient and Tamar picking up on the waves radiating from her sister suggested, 'I know, how about telling me tomorrow because we're all going to Pendrym aren't we? We can talk about it then.'

Nick sighed, 'Okay.'

In an attempt to lift his mood Tamar added, 'And you can tell me all about my growing fan base...'

But Morwenna wouldn't allow any further conversation. As far as she was concerned, Tamar leaving Porth Pyra was probably all Nick's fault. She'd never had much time for him and now he'd proved just how unreliable he could be, disappearing like that! It was probably his idea to go to Porth Talant in the first place however much Tamar might try to defend him.

And so a moment later Nick found himself being firmly shown to the door with his bag being thrust into his arms. The door was slammed closed as soon as he was outside, and he was filled with an unfamiliar gloom. If only he could have told Tamar about the eagle-woman then at least she would have been aware of the danger she was in. He looked around, scanning the festival crowds, and made his way slowly up the lane towards the main street but there was no sign of either the woman or of the crow, so maybe Tamar would be safe until they met again. He thought about what had just happened and then he remembered that they hadn't told Arthur what the man in the pub had said either. He put his hand in his pocket and was relieved that the dragon was still there. That was something anyway.

. . .

With his broad-brimmed hat pulled down over his eyes, a figure monitored Nick's progress up the street. On a roof, a dark-feathered bird cawed before swooping down onto the man's shoulder. The bird watched his master as he took something out of his pocket and smiling, tossed it into the air. The stone caught the light and the stranger nodded to a woman, dressed from head to toe in black.

The woman waited and watched Nick impassively as he threaded his way through the crowds and up the lane, before she left the dark doorway and walked towards the harbour. But the man glanced across to the cottage Nick had left moments before and smiled to himself; justice would be done.

Blood would be avenged.

Chapter 7

~ Time shift ~

Arthur stepped down into Kitto Cornish's cluttered shop in Pendrym. He took a few seconds to savour his surroundings. Ever since he'd first visited it a year ago, he'd never become bored with its shelves of books or chivalric models, and never minded if he'd had to wait for Gawain to finish serving a customer.

It was a dark and fusty place, more like a library than a shop. The ceiling was supported by warped, age-stained beams, and the bay windows displayed a chaotic jumble of holiday souvenirs. But Arthur's chief interest lay in the old books detailing the exploits of King Arthur and his knights, or those others discussing the finer points of chivalry. He'd lost count of the hours he must have spent leafing through them. By now his fingers recognised the textured linen or smooth leather covers, and the titles pressed into the spines. He could almost tell which book he was holding with his eyes closed. In fact he'd learnt so much about knights and chivalry and King Arthur's court that he thought he could almost write a book on it. For some reason, as the year had progressed, he'd felt a pressing urgency to get to know more about his namesake. King Arthur might be just a legend to some, but to Arthur Penhaligon he was as real as Gawain, Nick and Tamar.

The door closed and the old brass bell jangled, announcing his arrival. As the bell finished ringing a figure popped up from behind the counter with a feather duster in his hand and a pair of round glasses perched on the end of his nose. The shop owner checked the rest of the room, as if someone else might be lurking behind a display, before turning towards Arthur and bowing once. Arthur wished he wouldn't, it was so embarrassing.

'Sire,' the man said, 'I take it you are here to visit Gawain.'

'Yes Mr Cornish, he knows I'm coming,' Arthur replied.

'T'is always a pleasure to see you Sire... '

'Please,' Arthur said, 'please call me Art, or Arthur.'
He'd asked this before and knew what the answer would be. Ever since the previous summer, Gawain's uncle had insisted on addressing Arthur as 'Sire', because he was one of those who'd been present to witness Arthur's knighting by Excalibur.

'Oh I couldn't possibly, Sire.'

Gawain's uncle paused before suggesting, 'Would you prefer to be addressed as, 'Sir Arthur'?'

'No really, that wouldn't help at all!'

'Ah well,' Mr Cornish said, slightly crestfallen, 'then we will have to continue as before.'

He opened the door at the rear of the shop and stood to one side, bowing slightly, as Arthur passed him and headed up the stairs to the flat. Each footstep produced a tiny cloud of dust from the threadbare carpet; presumably Mr Cornish didn't worry about the private part of the building.

A heavily embroidered curtain hung at the top of the stairs. The embroidery depicted Cornwall and was scattered with pictures of pirates, swords and a castle. Arthur inspected it carefully. The sea was populated with dolphins and a seal was sewn swimming off the coast of Porth Talant. He peered more closely, he was certain that he hadn't seen that before. He hadn't noticed the castle either.

A voice came from the bottom of the stairs, 'Is everything alright Sire?'

'Yes I'm fine. I was looking at the curtain.'

'Ah, I *see*,' Mr Cornish said in a way that implied that he understood exactly what Arthur was looking at.

Then he muttered something to himself which Arthur could only just hear. He thought he heard Mr Cornish say, 'Everything will be revealed at its proper time.'

Arthur wondered if he was meant to reply but decided that he didn't know what to say anyway. So, pushing the curtain and his questions aside, he stepped into the living room and called out for his friend.

He was always fascinated with this room. It was crammed with pictures and ornaments, ticking clocks littered the floors and shelves - each one keeping a different time. Stacks of books, thick with dust, were piled high on the floor and in some cases nearly up to the ceiling. He glanced across to the hearth and almost wished he'd brought Lightning because the fire, as ever, was lit. Mr Cornish had a theory that it was always winter somewhere in the world - or in some time.

Then Gawain appeared at the bottom of another flight of stairs that led up to his room. 'You made it, then!'

'Yeah, no problem.'

'Have you seen anything else?'

'No,' Arthur said. 'Have you?'

Gawain shook his head, 'No, nothing; although I've still got the feeling that's something's about to happen.'

Arthur sank into a saggy armchair. 'Yeah, I know what you mean.'

'I wonder if the others have noticed anything,' Gawain said, glancing at his watch. 'Nick should be here soon. What about Tamar? I thought she was coming with you.'

'She was,' Arthur replied. 'But Morwenna won't let her out of her sight after yesterday, so she has to help out in the shop today. She started to try to tell me about that guy, Zephy...'

'Zephaniah?'

'Yeah him... and she said something about the sun disappearing and the moon coming out, but then Morwenna must have come in. So I still don't know what happened.'

'That sounds a bit weird,' Gawain said, and then a thought struck him. 'Hey, wasn't there a guy called Zephaniah who lived in Porth Pyra ages ago?'

'Don't know.'

'I'm sure there was, I think he was quite important.'

Gawain and Arthur glanced at one another but neither of them dared to voice the impossible.

Instead Arthur said, 'Dunno, history isn't my strong point mate.' He continued, 'At least Tamar's only missing the Town Criers competition.'

'That's true! Oh, I nearly forgot - I'd better go downstairs,' Gawain said. 'Nick will be here any minute and he can't cope with Uncle Kitto. In fact he sounded a bit on edge when he phoned this morning, but he said that he didn't want to go into details until we were all together.'

'That's not like him,' Arthur remarked. 'He's usually almost horizontal he's so laid back!'

'I know,' Gawain agreed, 'I was a bit surprised. Anyway there's loads of food, help yourself. Back in a minute.'

Arthur took in the plates of biscuits, stacks of sandwiches, sausage rolls and the chocolate cake, but it wasn't the food which attracted him. Instead, he reached towards a pile of books because there was one in particular which intrigued him.

This book was a dark midnight blue, with stars peppering the cover. In the centre of the picture a silver-haired knight on horseback was depicted brandishing a sword. Arthur looked at the book, carefully inspecting every detail. Oddly, it didn't have a title or an author's name, just a tiny image of a golden clock face on the spine. As he examined the picture of the clock, the room filled with chiming and the light flickered and darkened.

And Arthur was no longer in the armchair but standing alone; by a lake, on a moor.

Incredulous, he looked up at the night sky and at the moon and the stars. It was just like the cover of the book he'd been looking at. This was the most realistic dream he'd had in ages – because surely it *had* to be a dream.

Beating hooves drummed, filling the blue-black air, and as Arthur turned towards the sound he had a feeling that he knew who was approaching. And sure enough, galloping towards him was a knight on horseback, and his heart leapt because he knew that the figure wasn't a stranger but an old friend. It was Bedivere the aged knight Arthur had first met a year ago in such extraordinary circumstances; the knight who'd been the keeper of the sword, Excalibur.

'Sire!' exclaimed the knight as he brought his horse, whinnying and snorting, to a halt.

It was then that Arthur knew this wasn't a dream because he could smell the night air and the scent of warm horse.

'Sire,' Bedivere repeated, reaching down to clasp his hand, 'it's good to see you.'

The knight looked down at the boy, his deep-set eyes searching, far-seeing. 'You have grown in stature,' he stated.

Then smiling he added, 'And maybe in wisdom?'

'I'm not sure about the wisdom part!' Arthur replied. 'If I was wise I'd understand how I'm here instead of in Gawain's house. It can't be real... can it?'

Bedivere looked towards the night sky and mused, 'Art, there are times when our logical thoughts can be the enemy of all that is possible.'

'That doesn't help!' Arthur retorted.

Bedivere's eyes twinkled, but he quickly became serious, 'As much as I would wish to talk further on these matters, our time is limited and our meeting is for a purpose.'

Arthur sighed, 'Just like the last time.'

The knight nodded, 'Sadly, that is so.'

Arthur started to protest but Bedivere shook his head, 'Sire, suffice it to say that the object of your search will be found here.'

Puzzled, Arthur looked around at the bleak moorland and the silver lake. He wasn't searching for anything. Then he looked at Bedivere's side, there was no sword.

'The sword?' he asked.

Bedivere nodded, smiling slightly, pleased that Arthur had understood so quickly. 'Remember, she will be ready for you when you have need of her.'

'Will that be soon, then?'

'Ah Sire, as with my Lord before you, always questioning! I cannot furnish you with the answers.'

'It seems like I'm always only ever allowed to know a bit at a time,' Arthur said, frustration building despite the circumstances. 'I've been in a storm and heard voices of people who aren't even there; and I've been given a scroll and I can't read the writing. *And* now you're telling me that I'll need the sword and I've no idea what I'll need it for!'

Bedivere chuckled at this outburst but, instead of answering any of the questions, he said, 'When you have need of the sword you must think on our meeting and how it came about. Look beyond the frontispiece.'

'The front-is-piece?' Arthur asked.

A faint breeze swept across the moor. Bedivere looked up and around him, 'T'is time for us to go our separate ways.'

'Not already!' Arthur protested, dismayed that he'd been allowed such a brief meeting with his old friend.

'Aye Sire,' Bedivere replied softly. 'May good fortune pave your path. Heaven watches you.'

He leant down and offered his hand and now, when Arthur wished he had the right words, he couldn't think of anything to say.

Silently they clasped hands and Bedivere was turning his horse away and galloping into the distance across the moonlit moor.

Arthur watched him go and felt wretched. It only then occurred to him that maybe he could have asked whether they'd be granted another meeting.

. . .

Footsteps and voices tugged Arthur back and he was once more in an armchair in Kitto Cornish's sitting room, holding the book he'd been studying before being whisked away to a moorland night. Furthermore the clocks' chiming had been replaced by a gentle ticking; there was not even the slightest hint of what had just taken place.

Right now Arthur didn't want to talk to anyone, all he wanted was to hold on to the memory of that meeting.

So he closed his eyes and re-ran the conversation and tried to remember the last instruction Bedivere had given him. It had been something about the, 'front-is-piece', whatever that was.

Nick's face appeared around the curtain at the top of the stairs.

'Do I have your permission to enter, Sire?'

Arthur looked up and pulled himself back, 'Come in, idiot!'

Nick pushed the curtain and entered with a flourish, 'Hi, you made it then!'

Arthur nodded, 'Is Gawain there?'

'Yeah, he's coming up in a minute. He managed to stop his uncle do the bowing thing.'

'I haven't. He even offered to call me, 'Sir Arthur'!'

'Brilliant!' Nick said, grinning, and reached for a sandwich.

'And no, you can't call me that,' Arthur said.

Gawain came into the room, 'What can't he call you?'

'Oh nothing,' Arthur replied.

'Do you think it'd be a good idea if we called Arthur, 'Sir Arthur'?' Nick suggested to Gawain through the sandwich.

Gawain broke into a broad smile, 'Let me guess, Uncle Kitto.'

Arthur nodded but, although he'd been momentarily distracted, his thoughts were quickly back with Bedivere. The other two, watching him, saw the smile disappear to be replaced by a slight frown.

'What's up?' Nick asked, already onto the cake.

For a brief moment Arthur toyed with the idea of describing his experience to his friends, but instead he said, 'What's a front-is-piece?'

'Search me,' Nick replied, shrugging.

Gawain exclaimed, 'Oh, a frontispiece! It's at the front of a book, just inside the cover. It's usually a picture or something.'

'Oh right, I wonder… ' Arthur said to himself, and tried to open the star-speckled book, but it was fastened. A golden clasp held it tightly closed.

'Why would anyone want to lock a book?' he asked, frustrated.

'Dunno,' Gawain said. 'You'll have to ask Uncle Kitto.'

'Do you reckon he's got the key?'

Gawain shrugged, 'Ask him. What's so important anyway?'

'Oh just something somebody said. I'll ask him on our way out,' Arthur replied. He'd tell his friends about meeting Bedivere later. For now he wanted to keep the details of the midnight encounter to himself. He was afraid that if he tried to put it into words he would only destroy its memory; tear it into wisps which would float into the ether.

Instead he asked Nick, 'Wasn't there something you wanted to tell us?'

Since his arrival, Nick had been waiting for the right moment to tell his friends about the woman he'd seen watching Tamar, but Arthur's sudden preoccupation with the book had diverted his thoughts and he remembered the dragon-statue he'd found on the cliff path. He thrust the problem of Tamar's stalker aside, just for the moment, and dug deep into his pocket, 'Yes there was… I almost forgot to show you this!'

Gawain and Arthur tore themselves away from examining the book to see Nick holding up a carved, stone model of a dragon.

'Where did you get that?' Gawain asked.

'On the path from Porth Pyra. You know, when we were coming to your aunt's cottage,' Nick said to Arthur.

'It's almost the same as those stone models that Uncle Kitto has - except his are all knights and stuff – and yours is green.' Gawain said. 'I don't think he has any green carvings.'

'It is, isn't it?' Arthur agreed.

'D'you reckon it's important then?' Nick asked.

'Don't know,' Arthur said.

'I wonder what a dragon has to do with anything,' Nick mused.

Arthur studied it, 'I don't know. Like I've no idea what the scroll is about, or why it was so important for Tamar to deliver it to me... or why anyone would bother to lock a book!'

Nick and Gawain looked at each other and Nick raised his eyebrows.

It was unusual for Arthur to get wound up like this.

'Do you want to keep it?' Nick offered.

'No, it's okay mate,' Arthur said, shaking his head. 'I think it's meant to be for you. Just look after it for the rest of us.'

For a split second Nick looked pleased, then his expression clouded at the thought of the responsibility he'd been given.

He was used to taking the lead in some circumstances, but not when it came to looking after something that was probably valuable. He tucked the little statue deep into his pocket, under layers of wrappings and rubbish, and grabbed a chocolate-covered biscuit as a sort of comfort.

'Okay, if you're sure.'

Arthur turned to go and was at the top of the stairs when he stopped and asked Gawain, 'Do you think your uncle will let me borrow that book?'

Gawain grinned, 'He's not likely to refuse his Sire!'

'Oh shut up,' Arthur said, but despite himself he started smiling and, grabbing the book, led the way downstairs.

Chapter 8

~ The warning ~

The three boys stood with the crowds on Pendrym's promenade overlooking the town beach. A small stage had been erected and decorated with bunting in black and gold, Cornwall's colours, and hung with strings of lights. A hand-painted sign hanging above the platform declared, 'Town Crier of the Year'.

'Why would anyone want to do that?' Nick asked. 'It's a bit of a weird hobby, especially with all the dressing-up and stuff.'

'What, you mean you wouldn't want to get all dressed-up?' Gawain asked innocently.

Nick shuddered at the thought of the outfit that Tamar had made him wear. 'Look, can we forget about that? I was ambushed! It'll never happen again.'

Gawain grinned, but Nick was saved from further comments by a crackle from the loud speakers. 'Testing... one, two, three.'

There were a few ragged cheers as the presenter stepped forward.

'Ladies and gentlemen, we are delighted that so many of you have gathered for this most exciting of occasions. Pendrym is honoured to host the final of 'Town Crier of the Year'.'

There was a smattering of applause, mostly from the town councillors.

'Do you really want to watch this?' Nick remarked, but a woman standing beside him turned and glared, silencing any further comments.

Arthur shifted his backpack because the book was digging into him, he wondered what secrets it held. He'd gone into the shop ahead of the other two, so they hadn't witnessed Uncle Kitto's reaction when he'd seen Arthur holding the book. Neither had they seen him when Arthur had asked if he could borrow it.

At first he'd taken it from Arthur and stroked the cover. Then he'd peered closely at the clock on the spine, and murmured something about the hands having moved, before looking once more at the cover.

'So, the sword is gone!'

And Arthur had glanced at the knight, as he'd done earlier that afternoon, and felt his heart miss a beat. He'd known, without a doubt, that the knight had been carrying a sword, but now it had disappeared.

'That's impossible!'

At which Uncle Kitto looked up from examining the book and had said, 'Sire, surely you have been told that logical thought impedes all that is possible.'

'No, that's not quite what he said... ' Arthur had begun.

However Mr Cornish had started to smile and Arthur realised that he'd been tricked into revealing that Bedivere had spoken to him, when he'd been whisked from daytime in the sitting room to night-time on a lonely moor. And Arthur was instantly reminded of Bedivere and Michael; they both had that look about them too - a sort of all-seeing look.

'How did you know?'

Gawain's uncle had merely touched the side of his nose and winked, as Nick had burst through the door closely followed by Gawain.

'Oh, did Arthur ask you about the key to unlock the book?' Gawain asked.

'The key?' Gawain's uncle had said. 'Oh no, I haven't got it, but it will be found.'

Then he'd hurried to the front of the shop and, opening the door, looked out. Crowds had filled the street, lazily glancing at the shop windows while eating ice-creams, or posing for photos against the backdrop of the quaint Cornish town.

'You must make haste.'

Nick raised his eyebrows and looked at Gawain questioningly, but his friend had merely shrugged, 'Come on then.'

Gawain and Nick were already out in the lane as Arthur asked Mr Cornish, 'How will the key be found?'

But all he'd got in answer had been another brief wink and a serious, 'Kernow is for you, Sire. *Comero weeth.*'

. . .

A bell tolling roused Arthur from his thoughts. Nick dug him in the ribs and pointing to the stage, said, 'Honestly Art, who would want to look like that?'

Men, some tall, others short and round stood in a line. They were dressed in a wild mix of colours, in suits which generally included a sort of frock coat and a three cornered hat.

Arthur heard stifled giggles from Gawain and then an elderly lady leant forward, saying severely, 'My husband is number three!'

Straightaway their eyes were drawn to the third contestant, however instead of having the desired effect it only made matters worse. The woman's husband was the tallest and thinnest, and his appearance was the most eye-watering of all. Arthur had no doubt that the contestant's wife must have spent hours on her sewing machine creating the outfit for her husband. He concluded that the only logical explanation for that colour-combination must be that she was colour-blind. He was still trying to come up with a polite comment as Nick grabbed him and pulled him to the back of the crowd.

'Honestly mate, I thought I was going to explode,' he said. 'Let's go.'

Gawain shook his head, 'Purple and green, he looked like he'd got dressed in the dark!'

Nick and Gawain started giggling again and Gawain said to Nick, 'At least your blouse was white!'

'It wasn't a blouse, it was a shirt!' Nick objected.

'Yeah, right… don't believe everything Tamar tells you,' Gawain said, smirking.

But a voice cut across their debate, stopping them in their tracks. A familiar figure was standing on the stage, wearing a dark velvet frock coat. Along the edges of the sleeves, silver stars flickered, while the speaker's tricorn hat was embellished with more stars and moons, looking for all the world as if the outfit had been plucked from a midnight sky.

'Oh yay, oh yay, oh yay.'

It was Michael. The crowd was still. No one stirred, except for a dark-coated stranger who took a step back into the shadows.

Then Michael started to speak, 'T'is a glorious day when we're collected together to celebrate our Kernow and 'er heritage.'

The three friends glanced at one another and moved together towards the stage.

Michael continued, 'But know this; we're beset on every side by danger - and by those who would wish to do us harm.'

The judges were arranged along a table to the side of the stage, and were looking at one another, puzzled. This contestant wasn't on their list, and he was straying from the script the 'criers' had been given.

'We must all remember,' Michael continued, now looking directly at the three boys, 'that whatever happens, there be many gathered ready. For the past with the present and future entwine - providin' the perfect circle of time.'

'What did he say?' one of the judging panel asked, leaning across the table towards one of the other judges.

'I don't know, Ivor. I think it was somethin' 'bout the past and the present.'

'Who is he?' Ivor asked, looking around quizzically at his colleagues, but the other judges shook their heads.

None of them had been prepared for this eventuality.

Ivor raised his eyebrows and pushed his chair back, ready to intervene, but in that split-second their unannounced contestant had disappeared.

...

Servo, the Watcher, merged with the shadows and studied the crowd. Michael was on the stage while the three boys were forcing their way through to the front of the audience, desperate to get to him. However, there were also those other shadow-hunters waiting for their moment - biding their time.

He picked up his backpack, part of his walking camouflage, because he'd have to be ready for what was to follow.

He hoped that all was going well in Egypt with Jacob's son. Last time he'd been Watching, the boy had been wrongly imprisoned. It was difficult having to Watch so many years and miles apart. Viatoris only had to travel a few centuries – and just to Italy. But then a movement at the edge of the crowd caught Servo's eye, stilling his thoughts of that other time and place.

It was time to concentrate on Watching in this century.

. . .

Arthur pushed through the crowd to the back of the stage, but by the time he'd got there Michael had disappeared. He scanned the crowded promenade for any sign of his old friend but he'd vanished.

'Where is he?' Nick asked, catching up.

'Don't know, there's no sign of him,' Arthur replied. 'He must be here somewhere, he can't have just gone!'

Gawain had joined them, 'Can you see him?'

'It's impossible,' Nick muttered. 'He's just disappeared into thin air!'

'Logical thought is the enemy of all that's possible,' Arthur said, wondering why they hadn't been allowed to meet Michael.

'What?' Nick said.

'Oh, just something someone said to me,' Arthur replied.

'Why would he go, just like that?' Gawain puzzled. 'It's the sort of thing Uncle Kitto does, one minute he's there – the next he's gone.'

'Does he?' Arthur asked curiously. 'You never told us that.'

'Yeah, he's always done it, but I don't talk about it much,' Gawain said. 'I mean, our house is pretty weird at the best of times!'

Nick glanced at Gawain, 'You could say that, mate!'

Arthur sighed, 'Well, for whatever reason, Michael wasn't here to meet us, was he?' He thought for a moment, 'It must be to do with what he said.'

They were silent, considering Michael's speech.

'D'you think he was warning us?' Nick said.

'Yeah, maybe,' Gawain said thoughtfully. 'But I'm sure he was trying to tell us something else too.'

A dark shape flitted above their heads. Nick looked up and caught sight of a crow settling on a roof, and listened as it cawed once. Then he saw a figure, with his coat collar turned up and broad-brimmed hat tilted low over his face, standing a little way from them. It was the Crow Man. Nick nudged Arthur and nodded in their adversary's direction, but Arthur had already seen him. He'd also noticed a pale-haired man, accompanied by an albino dog - Matearnas's hound.

Chapter 9

~ Prisoner ~

Tamar was angry.

Working in Tremelin's ice-cream shop in Porth Pyra was never her idea of a good time, although the free chocolate-chip ice-cream was some compensation. But today she was all too aware of her friends together in Pendrym while she was stuck here by herself. No amount of ice-cream would make up for that. Helping in the shop had been Morwenna's idea of a punishment; a sort of payment for the worry she'd caused.

'You can't go off without telling me. Anything could have happened to you and I wouldn't have had a clue where you were!' she'd said.

'I wouldn't mind,' Tamar muttered to herself, as she cleaned out the ice-cream trays, 'but I didn't do anything wrong, and it wasn't *even* my fault.'

She scooped the last of the raspberry and honey ice-cream into a freezer box and slung the tray into the sink. She hated this job.

'*And* now she's gone off and left me to do all the cleaning up!'

She glanced up at the clock, only another quarter-of-an-hour and she'd be finished for the day. That was some consolation anyway.

The bell rang, announcing a customer, but as Tamar turned around her smile froze because an elderly couple were standing in front of the counter. They came in most days and she knew that they would spend ages choosing their ice-creams.

She sighed to herself, this was just her luck.

'There's so much to choose from, I never can make my mind up!' said the lady with a smile as she hovered in front of the counter. She started at one end of the display and carefully worked her way along, until she was finally on the point of deciding.

Tamar's hopes rose, perhaps this wouldn't take too long after all, but they were dashed as the woman turned to her husband.

'What are you going to have, Jack? You go first. I can't make my mind up!' Tamar's heart sank.

But Jack was equally indecisive and finally, before she lost the will to live, Tamar intervened.

'What about the pistachio? That goes really well with the vanilla and honeycomb ice-cream. It's my favourite combination!' she enthused, and crossed her fingers behind her back.

The woman's faced cleared, 'I would never have thought of that, what a good idea, we've never had that before! You are a clever young lady - isn't she Jack?'

Jack barely managed a word before his wife cut in again, 'It's the highlight of our day, coming for our ice-cream, isn't it Jack?'

This time her husband didn't even try to make a comment, instead he merely nodded his agreement. Tamar wasn't sure whether she felt more sorry for him never being allowed to say more than a couple of words, or whether her sympathies were with him over an ice-cream being the highlight of his day.

As they exited the shop the woman said, 'See you again tomorrow, dear.'

'No you won't,' Tamar murmured under her breath. 'There's no way I'll be here!'

She turned away to finish the last of her duties but the shop bell rang again and, with her heart sinking, she turned around. However this customer was unlike any she'd ever served before.

The shop windows misted over as crystals of ice spread across the glass, and the customer, a blond-haired woman dressed in black, took a couple of steps towards the counter.

'So, you have nearly finished the washing,' the woman said, her words sharply accented. 'That is good.'

Tamar took a step back as fingers of cold air reached out towards her.

'Can I help you?' she asked mechanically. The windows were now sheets of ice and a snowy mist rose from the ice-cream still lying in the chiller cabinet.

The woman smiled, inclined her head and looked at her in the same way as a cat looks at a bird or a mouse.

Her eyes widened and blinked just once, and her fingers twitched.

'Can you help me? I think, maybe, that you can.'

She stepped closer and suddenly Tamar was reminded of Matearnas. It could have been the way she bore herself, tall and straight-backed, or it may have been her appearance, with that hooked nose. Maybe it was the scent of old, attic clothes, wafting towards her on the icy air or the woman's commanding manner, but whatever the reason, Tamar's pulse was racing. Her heart thudded as she tried to control the rising panic but now she knew that it wasn't only the evidence of her eyes that gave her reason to be scared, but the evidence of her ears; because she'd heard those footsteps before, when she'd accompanied Zephaniah back through the centuries.

The woman smiled again, calmly assessing the situation. She knew that Tamar was alone.

'Yes,' the woman continued. 'You can help me. However I'm afraid that will mean that the work will have to be left unfinished.'

She glanced around the shop. 'I am certain that your sister will finish what is undone.'

The woman strode around the counter and Tamar caught a glimpse of the shoe that she'd last seen emerging under the arch when she'd been with Zephaniah. And before she was able to move away her wrist was being squeezed between ice-cold fingers and she was shivering as silver threads of frost crept along her arm.

Her stalker was dressed from head to foot in black velvet, the skirts brushing the floor, but it was her eyes that held Tamar. She'd heard it said that the eye is the window of the soul. If that was the case this woman didn't possess a soul.

'In answer to your question, yes, you are going to help me,' she smiled again. 'However, not to an ice-cream, I am quite cold enough.'

And the woman, firmly gripping Tamar's wrist, was steering her out of the shop as the little bell dolefully signalled their departure, and down the lane.

Tamar struggled to summon words, to shout out, but none came. The frost was seeping into her blood, creeping into her bones, and in the full sun of a summer's day, her teeth were chattering. She was being abducted in broad daylight in the heart of a bustling village, and no one was noticing. The woman strode down the lane, her grip freezing the flesh around Tamar's wrist, and smiled.

Under her breath she said, 'You will find it impossible to speak for a while but do not worry, it will not always be like this.'

Through the chill invading her brain, Tamar realised that she was being led to the harbour where a small fishing boat stood waiting.

'It is better not to struggle; your sister is not as safe as she could be.'

And with that threat ringing in her ears Tamar found herself being picked up and lifted into the boat. She looked at the quay. She was sure that someone would see what was happening but she could have been invisible. Not one person stopped or looked in her direction.

At that moment, as the boat's engine started up, a cottage door on the quayside opened and the fisherman who'd helped them through the 'Three Smugglers' came out. She wanted to shout but no words came and in the next instant she was being thrust into a tiny cabin and her abductor was picking up an old sack. The engine kicked in, sending her flying across the cabin to land heavily on the floor, and the sack was dropped over her head.

...

The Writer sat in a cottage in Porth Pyra overlooking the harbour and hoped that the Watchers were in place, because many witnesses would be needed for what was to follow. She dipped her pen in the inkpot. Most of the time the ink was green, very occasionally it was gold.

It had been gold on that extraordinary night almost a year ago when young Arthur had been named by the Sword. And now Excalibur was calling out to him again, she could feel it.

She glanced out of the window and watched the boat make its way out of the harbour with its captive on board. She'd seen Tamar led towards the craft, unable to escape from the woman's icy touch. They were clever she had to give them that, because not one person had stopped them. No one had intervened or tried to help the girl. The Writer frowned. There was no guarantee that Tamar Tamblyn would be rescued, no guarantee that she'd come out of this uninjured, or even alive.

Her thoughts turned to the book that she'd given to the boy, Nick, twelve months ago. She pondered on its contents and was fairly certain that she knew which page it would be choosing to display today, if anyone was there to see it. She'd entrusted it to his care knowing that she was taking a chance, yet even now she was certain that her trust would eventually be rewarded.

Looking across the harbour she saw the Watcher, Viatoris, turn towards the narrow lane that led to the cliff path and saw that he was still wearing those ridiculous shoes. She sighed and shook her head. Still, the other Watcher, Servo, should be at Pendrym by now, ready to witness all that might happen there.

Sliding her glasses onto her nose, the string dangling around her neck, the Writer started to Write, but her hand faltered when she saw the colour of the ink the pen had chosen. Blood-red words were creeping across the page in front of her, forming before the pen Wrote them. Red, the colour of danger.

. . .

Bumping from one side of the cabin to the other, wrapped in the heavy sacking, Tamar heard the note of the engine change. The boat was gaining speed as it bounced across the top of the waves. Tamar concentrated on saving herself from being flung into the various sharp corners which had already made their mark on her arms and legs, while a memory tried to elbow its way into her mind.

The engine note dropped, the boat slowed and Tamar was slung over a bony shoulder with the sacking pulled so tightly over her face that she thought she might suffocate. Panicking, and with the blood rushing to her head, she kicked out, but her feet were caught in a vice-like grip.

'Now, now,' said a gruff voice. 'We can't be 'aving anyone 'urt can we?'

She heard the voice ask, 'Where do you want 'er, Mistress?'

Tamar didn't hear the answer and it was impossible to tell where she was being taken, although it felt as though they were climbing. But just as she thought they'd gained level ground she was thrown, and was falling, tumbling through space.

Seconds later – or maybe only spit-seconds - and she was crashing into a hard, un-giving surface with her shoulder taking the full impact of the fall. She lay stunned, overwhelmed by the pain radiating out from her shoulder. She couldn't have moved if she'd wanted to because someone had tied the neck of the sack. Her heart drummed in her ears as she tried to breathe and waves of pain washed over her. Tamar swallowed. She was in a giant bubble of sickness and fear. This sort of thing didn't happen in real life, it just happened in books, didn't it? Tamar had always prided herself on her resilience. She'd always thought of herself as brave and self-sufficient but now she was just plain scared, and she was hurting, a lot. She was vaguely aware of some sort of animal sounds on the other side of the sacking but she didn't care what was there. Dust filled her eyes and mouth, she hurt and ached and her ears buzzed and all she wanted was to be at home with her mum. A sob rose and escaped.

On the other side of the sack a wet nose sniffed suspiciously and circled the parcel that had landed at its feet, but at the first whimper it sprung back with its snout quivering and its ears on full alert.

There was another whimper and a tiny groan from whatever was within the sacking. This was much too interesting and the animal's curiosity got the better of it. Once again it crept forwards, slowly edging closer to the bundle and sniffed, and its senses were filled with the scent of a human - and of blood. Now its curiosity was really aroused, and the creature nervously stole around the sack, ready to retreat if it was attacked.

A cry came from inside the bundle, and a gnarled finger tapped the dog as an impatient voice ordered, 'Back dog. Leave it be.'

But the dog took no notice of the command. There were too many interesting scents and noises.

'Darn dog, I be tellin' you - leave it be!'

There was a whimper and a word from inside the parcel, but the owner of the finger couldn't make out what was said. He leant forwards, holding on to the dog, trying to make out the words. Eventually he mumbled something and, clanking, shuffled forwards.

Gripping the rope that bound the open edge of the sack, he took out a rusty knife, hooked it under the rope and started to saw until it finally fell open.

Three pairs of eyes surveyed one another.

Tamar's first sight of her companions was alarming. One was a man. He had dark eyes which squinted through black, wiry hair, and he was sporting an immense beard which curled and grew from beneath his eyes to finish up somewhere below his waist. He moved, trying to make himself comfortable, and a glint caught her eye. She glanced down to his ankles and saw that he had an iron shackle clamped around each leg, chaining him to the floor. It seemed that he was also a prisoner. Meanwhile a long-snouted animal, as furry as the face was hairy, sat panting beside the man with its tongue spilling out of its mouth between rows of sharply pointed teeth.

The hairy face made a sound.

Tamar couldn't make it out. If her ears had been working properly, she would have heard it say, 'Ah, so it be a girl who 'as been sent to us. I was thinkin' it would be a boy!'

The animal sidled forwards again. Tamar whimpered and closed her eyes. Perhaps they would leave her alone if she lay still.

But a memory had been stirred by that whimper and, before its companion was able to stop it, the dog was covering Tamar in a glistening layer of saliva.

'Yuck, stop!' she groaned, shrinking back into the sack. But the animal was on a mission. This pup wasn't well.

'Dog, leave 'er be,' said Hairy Face. Then he mumbled a couple of words which Tamar recognised, '*Comero weeth.*'

Chapter 10

~ Challenged ~

Pendrym

On Pendrym promenade, Arthur, Nick and Gawain had formed themselves into a tight triangle, each looking out towards their adversaries. Arthur was acutely aware of the book hidden in his backpack, and he had a sickening feeling that both the Crow Man and the Pale Stranger were aware of it as well.

He looked around. They were cornered. The river was at their back, the Crow Man was covering the lane leading back to the town and the Pale Stranger was blocking the route towards the beach. The middle ground was held by the dog - if you could call it that. The dog's eyes watched Arthur hungrily, waiting to be given the order to attack. In its dull mind he knew that this human had something to do with the death of his mistress, Matearnas.

The Pale Stranger smiled, and Arthur recalled the evening when they'd all been made Guardians and he'd been made the Guide. He remembered holding the sword high above his head, and his promise to protect Cornwall and its people. And he was reminded of Nick's words when he'd caught sight of the Pale Man among those assembled to witness Excalibur knight the Guardians. Nick had said something about not wanting to meet the Pale Stranger on a dark night. Well, it wasn't night, and there were people around, but to all intents and purposes they were alone against their enemies.

As he was thinking this the Crow Man glanced across to the Pale Stranger and, together, they looked at the sky. There was a pulse of lightning and a rumble of thunder and the people around them began to hastily collect their bags and belongings, hurriedly making for the shelter of coffee shops and cafés. The town criers and the committee, seeing the crowds disappear, quickly conferred and decided to wait until the storm was over before they continued the contest and they too left the stage. Arthur and his friends were alone, on the rain-soaked promenade.

Nick said under his breath, 'Okay, what do we do now?'

Gawain muttered, 'No idea.'

Nick said to Arthur, 'Think I was right about the Pale Guy.'

Arthur nodded, but all the while his mind was in overdrive trying to come up with a way out. Gawain looked from one man to the other and saw that their eyes were focused on Arthur and his backpack. They wanted Arthur - and Gawain had a sudden realisation that they knew about the book.

Gawain murmured, 'You've to get out of here, Art. I think they know what you've got in your backpack.'

'There's no way I'm leaving you guys,' Arthur said, sounding a lot braver than he felt. He wasn't a hero and he knew it. So did the Crow Man.

While they'd been talking, their adversaries had been casually edging forwards. No one watching would have any idea that anything out of the ordinary was happening, and the dog was tensing, ready to spring.

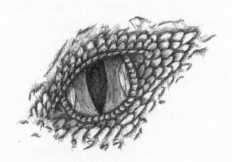

'Nick, the dragon, have you got it?' Arthur asked, an idea and a hope taking shape.

'Yeah, it's in my pocket, d'you want it?'

'No, he's asking out of curiosity,' Gawain hissed. 'Course he wants it!'

'Okay!' Nick retorted and dug the statue from his pocket. Smoothly, he palmed it and slipped it behind his back to Arthur.

'Thanks mate,' Arthur said, grabbing it.

And at that instant there was an explosion of energy and the dog flew, leaping, its teeth bared. But Arthur had the dragon in his hand and whipping it out, held it high above him. A jet of flame shot out of the dragon's mouth as the dog reared up. There was a yelp and a thud and the dog lay on the ground, stunned, and the rain, which had been falling steadily since that first crack of lightning, stopped. The Crow Man and the Pale Stranger froze in their tracks.

No one moved and it was then that Arthur heard the words.

Well perhaps not *heard* them, so much as *felt* them. They were a river of red-hot anger burning into his brain and immediately Arthur understood what the words would be if they were spoken - and they weren't polite.

The Crow Man fixed him with a look that matched the words, a look bursting with loathing, and in that instant Arthur knew that the Crow Man meant business and he understood every un-said word. They were telling him that next time he wouldn't be so fortunate and that he wouldn't be able to escape. He'd escaped once before, and maybe he would now, but he was being told that he wouldn't escape a third time. Arthur glanced quickly at Nick and Gawain but, from the relief on their faces, it was obvious that they hadn't heard the words – or seen the dragon's actions.

From behind him there was a gruff, 'Well, we'll see about that, won't we?'

They spun around. There, with his arms folded, was the fisherman who'd rescued Nick and Tamar in Porth Pyra at 'The Three Smugglers' pub. He was watching the Crow Man as the Pale Stranger started to edge away.

His eyes narrowed and he spoke to the Pale Man, 'So, this isn't the place assigned for the fight, Hagarawall? Well if it's not here, I'm thinking I know where it'll be. I'll be ready because, *theram cara Kernow*! (I love Cornwall!)'

This stopped the Crow Man in his tracks and this time, although he could feel the heat burning into his brain, Arthur couldn't hear the words. However watching the fisherman's face, he knew he'd understood them and didn't like what he'd heard.

He replied in words they could all hear, 'That's a strange kind of loyalty Brane. T'is a twisted world you be livin' in. *She* turned you from what is right.'

Then he gestured towards Arthur, 'This one 'ere, this boy be the rightful heir, not your made-up queen.'

This time the Crow Man's fury made Arthur's brain boil, and he clutched his head. The fisherman looked at Arthur and back towards the Crow Man.

'That'll do,' he commanded. 'You go on your way. We'll meet again dreckly.'

The boys waited while both the Crow Man and the Pale Stranger stood, undecided. The odds were in their favour: two men and a dog against one man and some boys. But Arthur was still clutching the stone dragon. The Crow Man's eyes locked onto it and then flicked down to the dog, cowering beside him. A pulse of energy swept through Arthur's brain as the Crow Man's frustration and anger hammered inside his head. But the Pale Stranger had made his decision and, gesturing to his companion, turned away with the dog trailing behind him.

The Crow Man glanced after his ally and then back towards the boy, and his eyes narrowed. He didn't say a word, he didn't need to. Instead he just sent another stream of molten rage into Arthur's brain before throwing a defiant look towards the fisherman. Finally, pulling his hat down over his eyes, he turned away but Arthur knew that it wouldn't be long before the pair made their next move.

The boys and the fisherman watched them go. No one spoke until they were out of sight but as the trio rounded the corner Nick breathed a sigh of relief.

'Boy, I thought we'd had it!'

Gawain nodded, 'So did I.'

Arthur didn't answer. His head was agony.

Gawain watched his friend thoughtfully. He could see that something had happened to Arthur. He looked awful.

But Nick's attention had switched to their rescuer, 'Where did you come from?' he asked.

The fisherman's lips twitched and he raised an eyebrow, 'Boats go awful well on water.'

Nick and Gawain peered over the harbour wall. A rusting, vertical ladder was attached to the stones with a boat tied to one of the rails.

'Yeah but, I mean how did you...'

''ow did I what?' the fisherman prompted him.

'Well, how did you know to turn up then?' Nick finished.

Their rescuer merely smiled, and each one of them was reminded of Michael Jolly, at which moment he repeated a phrase they'd heard before.

'There's sometimes a direct means for knowing when 'elp is needed.'

Arthur was staring at the boat. Below the prow a pair of dark eyes met his and this time he knew that he wasn't mistaken. It was the same seal. The one he'd met last summer. The one which had helped him save little

Kensa from drowning. His head was pounding - the Crow Man's fury had made its mark, but he looked curiously at the fisherman.

'That's the same... ow!' he said, and stopped, clutching his head.

'What's up?' Gawain asked.

'My head, it feels like it's going to burst,' Arthur replied. Even speaking was painful. He felt as if he was going to be sick.

The fisherman looked at Arthur.

'You're staying at Dywana's aren't you?'

Arthur nodded, wondering how he knew.

'Lads,' he said to Gawain and Nick, 'I'm going to take your friend back home. You'll be safe enough, but you must stay together.'

'Too right, we will!' Nick exclaimed, retrieving the now-lifeless statue from Arthur's hand.

Arthur wanted to tell Nick what the dragon had done but he couldn't summon the words. Neither of the other two seemed to have noticed its part in their rescue.

'You know what Nick,' Gawain started, 'I think it may be an idea if you stayed at mine. Strength in numbers and all that.'

Nick's face lit up.

'Yeah, that'd be great but..' he paused, 'do you think you could ask your uncle not to do the little bowing thing?'

Gawain grinned. How was it that Nick could so quickly lighten the atmosphere just by being him?

'I'll see if I can persuade him.'

The fisherman, satisfied with this arrangement said to Gawain, 'Say, '*durdathawhy*' to Kitto for me.'

'Say what?'

'It means 'good day'. Tell him John Oliver sends his greetings and we'll meet at the lake when the hour comes.'

Nick was looking puzzled, 'How come you know Gawain's uncle?'

But before there was time for an answer another thought hit him, 'I *knew* I'd seen you before! You were the man at the pub, weren't you? Those are some tattoos you've got.'

The fisherman smiled.

'Yes, that was me in Porth Pyra and as for Kitto - we've been friends for longer than you'd believe. I knew Kitto afore this one was born,' he said, indicating Gawain.

'Did you? I didn't know that,' Gawain said, looking puzzled. He couldn't remember ever having seen him.

John Oliver cut short any further conversation, 'You're both safe enough for the time, but it'd be better if you were on your way to Kitto's now.'

He turned to Arthur who was unusually quiet, and whose face was still a pale shade of green.

'Now lad, t'is time for you to go back to Dywana's; I can feel her worry building from here and that's not a good feelin'.'

And before Arthur had time for a word he was being ushered down the rusty ladder and into the waiting boat.

John Oliver caught sight of a shadow waiting and Watching. He saw it peel away from the cover of the lifeboat house and mingle with the crowds, ready to follow Nick and Gawain. John Oliver was fully aware of the Rule, even so he was comforted to know that the lads weren't entirely alone, and he knew that they'd be fine when they were at Kitto's place.

. . .

There was a gentle swell but the storm of a short time before had cleared, leaving the sun sinking in a clear blue sky shot through with pink. A couple of seagulls flew overhead, following the boat. Arthur looked at the roofs of the cottages lining the quay, but there was no sign of the crow and he began to relax.

He switched his attention to the man who'd rescued them and looked at the tattoos winding up his arms. Seeing the seal etched in the man's nut-brown skin reminded him of the eyes he'd seen a few moments before.

'There was a seal here, wasn't there?'

John Oliver merely nodded, one hand on the tiller, as he guided the little boat out of the river towards the open sea.

'Last year,' Arthur said, 'I rescued a little girl from this river... I didn't do it alone, a seal helped me. Do you think it could be the same one?'

'Could be,' he replied. 'In fact I'd say it's more than likely.'

Arthur sat back on the wooden bench and looked over the side but the animal had disappeared. Both man and boy were silent but as he started to feel better more questions were starting to pile up. Sometimes Arthur wished that his brain would give it a rest; he bet other people had minds that would shut down but his always seemed to be on the go.

'You know back then, when you talked to the Crow Man, could you feel the words too?'

John smiled, 'I could 'feel' them, yes.'

Arthur picked up a piece of rope lying beside him and fed it through his fingers while he thought. His brain felt as though it had been pulped and the headache was still nagging.

'So,' he mused, 'you could hear, feel his words… and I could, but Nick and Gawain couldn't.'

John Oliver nodded.

'Why could *I* hear them? I've never had anything like that happen to me before.'

'What else 'as happened today?'

The boat turned to follow the coast, back to Dywana's. Further out to sea, Lemayne Island was emptying the last of its day-trippers into the glass-bottomed boat and a tall-masted ship sailed behind the island.

Arthur looked sideways at John Oliver, 'Quite a lot, I've seen two old friends that I haven't seen in a while…' He trailed away, reluctant to add anymore because, after all, he'd only met this man a few minutes before.

Dolphins circled the boat as it puttered around the headland but Arthur was unaware of their escorts and leant back, considering all that had happened since that morning.

The fisherman nodded approvingly at Arthur's answer, 'You're learning already; only trust them you know.'

He glanced around him and over the side of the boat into the clear waters below and Arthur, following his gaze, caught sight of the creatures accompanying the boat.

'Awesome!' Arthur said softly, afraid that he might scare them off.

He turned around ignoring the dull ache triggered by any move, and knelt up on the bench.

'They're fantastic!'

He grinned at the fisherman, all doubts banished. If ever there was a sign of approval, this was it.

He leant over and dipped his hand deeper into the water and one of the dolphins swam up to him and touched his hand. Arthur was mesmerised.

'They know their Sire,' the fisherman said.

Arthur leant further over, lost in the moment. One by one, each dolphin took it in turn to swim up to the boy, touch his hand, and swim away. With each touch Arthur felt more reassured and his grin grew, there was a sort of *click* in his head and he suddenly found himself saying words he didn't even understand, '*Tereba nessa!*'

And there was an explosion of light and water. One of the animals leapt out in a perfect arc, sprinkling Arthur with ice-cold water and disappeared, trailing the others after him. He watched the last one go and turned to John Oliver.

'That was amazing!' His headache was gone. 'Brilliant! But... *tereba nessa*... I don't even know what it means!'

The fisherman adjusted their course slightly, avoiding the rocks hidden below the water.

'*Tereba nessa*, till next time,' he said as if it was perfectly normal to find yourself speaking in a language you didn't know.

'T"is the ancient tongue, you'll be findin' other words in time. Now, if I'm right, you've seen Michael and Bedivere, and done a bit of deep listenin'. Brane back there was usin' it all wrong but he's always been a hot-headed one; even afore he took the wrong path.'

'Brane?'

'T"is the old word for crow.'

'Oh, the Crow Man!'

'That's your name for him.'

Arthur nodded, trying to assimilate all that he'd been through, 'You knew I'd seen Bedivere too?'

John Oliver glanced at him and the backpack lying on the boards of the boat.

'Mmm, but that's not my business. Right now what's important is for you to be learned 'ow to control the deep listenin'. It'll burn you up if you let it 'ave its way. Mostly there's no problem because folks generally use it for the good, then there's no heat in it, but you'll 'ave to practise.'

'But I don't even know what to do!'

'Quiet then an' listen,' his teacher said firmly.

There was silence then, apart from the boat's engine and the gulls overhead. Arthur waited for John Oliver to explain but instead of spoken words, unsaid phrases were sidling into his mind. Words which were far more precise and beautiful than any spoken out loud. He didn't need to hear them spoken to understand what was being said.

Arthur grinned from ear to ear, 'That's brilliant! How do you do it?'

'You try,' the fisherman said.

Arthur closed his eyes and frowned, focusing all his energy on the words he wanted to say.

'Steady boy, you'll explode if you do it like that! T'is easy, think them words an' I'll hear them.'

So Arthur started. At first he tried to think of particular words but then he understood that something deeper was happening. The individual words were being replaced by pictures and colours, unrestricted by mere language. Very soon he was telling John Oliver all about his meeting with Bedivere; the day becoming night, and his anguish at having to be parted from his old friend so soon after meeting him.

He opened his eyes to see the fisherman watching him and, without a spoken word being said, knew that his teacher had heard and understood every thought and emotion he'd silently expressed.

Neither of them uttered another word, they didn't need to, and by now they were heading back inland towards the little bay. A figure was standing on the beach waiting for them with a black and white dog by her side.

John Oliver grinned and said, 'Go on surprise 'er.'

'What, do you mean use the deep words?'

The man nodded, grinning broadly, a mischievous glint in his eye.

Arthur looked at Dywana and thought, very carefully.

Beside him the fisherman chuckled as he caught the stream of questions and exclamations flying back to them from Dywana. He glanced at Arthur and watched as he too received the barrage of unspoken words from his aunt.

Arthur grinned as his brain was filled with the most intense colours. At first they were mostly indigo and scarlet, threaded through with a little silver and gold. They were a jumble of questions, statements and exclamations, mixed with some scolding for John Oliver for daring to spring this surprise on her, but eventually they settled down. And then his Aunt Dywana was welcoming him as one who'd been honoured, because this special gift was very rarely given, and certainly not to one so young.

Chapter 11

~ Secret revealed ~

Tamar crouched at the other side of the space, concentrating on keeping a distance between herself and Hairy Face and the dog. Her shoulder was agony but she was determined to maintain a hold on the situation. She'd given herself a good talking to, and had forced back the tears that had threatened to overwhelm her. At least she could breathe easily again, now that she was released from the sack, and that put a whole new perspective on her situation. She was still a prisoner, and still in pain, but it was just about manageable. She had to remember that she was a Guardian appointed by Excalibur and she was determined to show that she was worth the trust invested in her.

The dog started to creep forwards again, but Tamar had had enough of her ministrations and she glared at it until the animal shrank back. Few people, let alone animals, would have the courage to ignore those eyes.

Hairy Face had started to speak but Tamar was still having trouble making out the words.

'Is you hurt, lass?'

He shuffled a little closer but was immediately stalled by a glare.

Holding up his hands, he said, 'It's alright, I'll stay 'ere.' And he sat back against the wooden wall and rearranged his shackled legs into a slightly more comfortable position.

Tamar waited until the man had settled on the opposite side of the space, and the dog was lying down, before she took her eyes off them.

She surveyed her surroundings, but there wasn't much to see. The walls were wood-panelled and undecorated, except for one which had a circular, shiny brass disc fixed at head-height. There were no chairs, or furniture of any sort: no rugs, lights or pictures, no windows or doors, just a pile of old sacks piled in one corner and a cracked bowl for the dog's water. In fact she realised that the only entrance appeared to be an open square in the ceiling above them, so it was no wonder her shoulder was hurting because her captors must have dropped her through this ceiling-door. Looking up she could see the sky, but nothing else to give her any idea of where she was. Her ears buzzed and whenever she tried to concentrate on anything her vision became blurred. She closed her eyes again. Maybe she'd feel better if she slept.

A shadow flickered above them, someone was blocking the light from the square, but Tamar didn't care who was there. She wanted to sleep and the pain to go away. She lay down on the bare, wooden boards with her back to the panelled wall and curled up. She could hear voices - but again couldn't make out any words, anyway she didn't care what they were saying. She'd used up all her reserves of energy keeping Hairy Man and the dog at bay.

The man watched her slip into a troubled sleep and a frown slipped across his face.

'They've hurt 'er, they'll pay for that,' he said quietly to himself.

He glanced up at the square and listened to the conversation above him. Two voices, one a man, the other a woman, were having a heated discussion. He could only make out snippets and the occasional phrase but there was a definite disagreement.

'So, you were defeated by one man and a tiny, stone dragon!'

A male voice muttered something in reply before the female carried on mockingly, 'No, I am sure I would have found a pocket-sized statue equally terrifying.'

This time the male voice said something about John Oliver and the frown on the listener's face vanished to be replaced by a knowing smile.

But now the male voice was raised and the woman appeared to be justifying something she'd done. 'It was the only way. Time is short and we need the girl - especially as you have been unable to secure the prize.'

The two must have started to move away because their voices became fainter and, try as he might, their eavesdropper couldn't catch any more of their argument.

He looked up at the ceiling, as if to ensure that no one was there, and put his hand to his chest. Slowly he withdrew a silver chain from his jacket pocket hidden beneath his dense, black beard. Again, he checked the square above him before pulling the chain fully out. A fat, silver disc emerged dangling on the silver links. It twisted and turned and caught the light, splitting it into fine, bright shards of broken beams which sliced through the dusty gloom. One side of the disc was engraved with words and pictures which swirled and coiled around each other, while the other side glittered with perfect green emeralds. He held it up to the light, smiling with satisfaction. Then he put it to his ear, listened intently, heard a muffled chime and nodded.

The ancient pocket watch ticked, marking the seconds and minutes until it was handed to its new owner. It calmed its hands and adjusted its face. It was over two hundred years since it had been held by its last Keeper, and since they'd travelled through time together. What difference would a few more hours or days make? It chimed once – it could feel the Time Keeper nearby – not long now.

'They'd be proper mad if they knew that such a treasure be 'idden right under their noses!'

The watch's custodian chuckled and tucked the chain and its treasure back in his pocket, and carefully rearranged his beard to cover any trace of what lay hidden there.

. . .

Lemagne Island

On the cliffs high above Porth Talant a figure stood Watching. From here Viatoris could see Lemayne Island and the tall-masted ship lying on the horizon.

He'd also witnessed the little boat carrying John Oliver and the boy towards Porth Talant. He'd Watched the dolphins and he'd seen the colours explode above Arthur's head. So, the boy was being acknowledged by both man and animal, *and* he'd been taught the deep talking and listening. That could only mean one thing – he must have been to the Other Place. The Place where the sword waited.

Viatoris looked down at his shoes as he felt the pull through the years. He knew that Leonardo's time in Italy was calling, but he looked out to sea and wondered if the girl was safe. Again he thought about the Rule and the difficulty of observing events and never being allowed to intervene. Of course he understood the reasoning behind the Rule, and the insistence that all the Watchers should follow this instruction, but there were occasions when he wished for just a *little* flexibility.

The pull was getting stronger. He couldn't wait and Watch any longer on this cliff, in this century, he had to go. He looked at the little bay below him, now empty of people, and for the first time Viatoris realised that this place was untouched by modern times and a dangerous thought took root.

'I wonder!' he mused to himself. 'Now surely that wouldn't do any harm?'

He cast a quick look around and moved into the shadows. A tiny crackle like static electricity, a *'woomph'* - and he was gone.

. . .

On the edge of the sandy bay, in her low-roofed cottage, Arthur's aunt was bustling about the kitchen. As usual her first concern was ensuring that anyone under her roof was properly fed. So without consulting her nephew, she'd retrieved the cake tin and cut a couple of slices of cake (lemon this time), and thrust a plate across the table to him. She didn't need to be told that he needed a few minutes of quiet before they could begin to discuss what had happened. Once she was satisfied that he was settled she turned her attention to her shelf of jars and bottles.

Starting at one end of the shelf, she began to work along it, inspecting each and every one. Some she rotated a quarter-turn, others she would gently shake and one or two were left untouched. She carried on like this until she arrived at a dusty, green glass bottle which appeared to require more thorough investigation. Cautiously she tipped it and, holding it up to the light, peered through the murky glass. It blipped once and she loosened the cork in its neck, pulled it out and dipped her finger into the mixture. Then she swirled the bottle and sniffed the contents. Arthur caught the tiniest suggestion of raw honey and warmed cider before Dywana pushed the cork firmly into the neck of the bottle and turned her attention back to Arthur.

'So,' Dywana said, 'John 'as been teaching you the deep listenin'.'

'Yes,' Arthur answered, still a little overwhelmed by all he'd experienced. 'It was difficult at first, but then it just sort of happened. I hardly had to do anything, just think!'

Dywana glanced across the room to the painting. 'T''is a rare gift,' she said. The knight in the frame nodded silently, agreeing, and the seal on the windowsill blinked.

Arthur picked at the few crumbs left on his plate, oblivious to those others involved in the conversation, and speculated on what he'd been taught. 'One thing puzzles me though, if you can do that, why do you bother with ordinary words at all?'

But instead of answering his question, Dywana pulled out a chair, sat down and asked, 'Remember last year, when you were in the Granite House?'

Arthur nodded.

'And when you were at Michael and Angela's?'

Arthur frowned. He couldn't see where this was leading.

'Do you?' she asked again insistently.

'Yes, of course I do!' This was just like talking to Bedivere. Those conversations never went in a straight line either.

'Well, unless I'm mistaken, you might 'ave heard the singing.'

Arthur thought carefully and remembered the Crow Man trying to give him that drink and the glass shattering, spilling the contents and the 'singing'. He also recalled Bedivere's reaction when he'd heard it, and the smile that had lit up his face.

'Yes, I did.'

Dywana waited, observing Arthur's reaction to the memories of that day, and explained, 'Well, the singing and the deep thinkin' are both from the same place. They're a sort of promise, or a token, of what lies waiting for us. It's to be handled with care.'

Arthur said, 'D'you mean it's not for everyday use?'

Dywana nodded.

But Arthur hadn't finished, 'How can the Crow Man do it? I mean it was agony when he was doing the deep thinking.'

Dywana was silent and glanced at the painting of the knight on the wall as if she was looking for guidance. Arthur didn't notice the knight smile and nod once again.

She sighed. 'The thing is Art, t'was a gift given to Brane and he can choose how to use it. Brane has taken a different path but he still 'as the freedom to use the gift as he wishes.

Arthur thought about the explosion of sound in his head when the Crow Man had become angry at John Oliver and remembered that the colours had been dark - not the rainbow of colours he'd experienced when talking to John and Dywana.

'Can other people, you know other people who have the gift, can they sort of tune into it too? I mean... can everyone who can deep talk join in every conversation?'

She shook her head, 'No, t'is only 'eard by them who is meant to hear.'

'Well how was I able to hear the Crow Man, Brane, when it was aimed at John?'

'Sounds to me like he was proper furious and sometimes, if the thinker is right at the edge of some feeling like anger, it can leak out.'

Arthur finished the cake that had appeared on his plate and pushed his chair back and thought for a few minutes. This was a lot to take in. Lightning sat up expectantly.

'No boy, no walk.'

He picked up his backpack and looked at the knight in the painting, it bore an uncanny resemblance to the photo of Great-Uncle Lance he'd got. Why hadn't he noticed that before? Dywana watched him but said nothing.

'Thanks for the cake... and everything,' Arthur said as he made for the door. 'I'm just going upstairs, there's a couple of things I need to find out.'

Dywana didn't question him as his parents might have done. She understood his world. She also understood that he had to be left alone to do some of the finding out for himself.

Arthur closed the bedroom door behind him, slung the backpack on the shabby armchair and pulled the bed away from the wall to reveal a tiny, painted door set into the wall. There was just enough room to lever it open. Reaching into the cobwebby space he pulled out a battered cardboard box plastered with layers of stickers, souvenirs of places he and his parents had visited on their holidays. It felt as if ordinary things like family holidays were a hundred miles away now.

'Sit down boy,' he said to Lightning. 'We're not going anywhere for a while.'

The dog climbed into his basket, turned around once, curled up, and within seconds was sound asleep.

Arthur opened his backpack and took out the book and examined the cover again. The sword had definitely disappeared but the knight was still in the same place and the stars still shone. He looked at the clock on the book's spine. Tiny angels stood at each corner of the clock's face, just as they had on Michael and Angela's grandfather clock in their moorland cottage.

Putting the book to one side, Arthur lifted the box lid. Two miniature statues of knights lay among the leaflets and badges he'd collected at school and on outings. One of the statues had been a gift entrusted to him by Great-Uncle Lance; the other had been given to him by Mr Cornish last year before the night of the Commissioning.

'You stay there guys,' he said to them. 'I don't need you for the minute.'

Instead he picked up the scroll which he'd carefully tucked into the edge of the box.

'Now, will you be any clearer?' he said as he untied the ribbon.

Unrolling the scroll, Arthur caught himself holding his breath, wondering if he would understand any of the words.

The hilt of the sword was clear enough but the letters still swam across the parchment. He'd wondered if the book and the scroll might have worked together in some way but the words were still unclear, and he didn't have a key to the book.

'So that's a 'no' then,' Arthur muttered to himself, but as he leant forward his chain swung towards the book. He glanced down to the clasp firmly holding the book closed, and then back to the sword and chain swinging around his neck, and an idea began to grow.

'I wonder...' he said to himself.

And slipping the chain over his head, he grasped the miniature sword and slotted it into the minute key hole. He turned it, and with a 'click' the clasp sprang apart and the book opened at the first page.

He didn't know what he'd been expecting to see, but it certainly wasn't that!

Chapter 12

~ Dragon's fire ~

The clocks ticked and the fire burned steadily in Kitto's cottage in Pendrym.

'How can you put up with a fire in summer?' Nick asked.

'I've grown up with it,' Gawain answered easily, 'it's always been one of Uncle Kitto's things.

They looked around at the room and once again Nick was struck by the *otherness* of Gawain's home. He was sure that the books rearranged themselves from time to time when they felt it was time to be read. Then he noticed a clock that he hadn't seen here before, it was a grandfather clock.

'You've got the Jolly's clock!' he exclaimed.

Gawain looked up, 'Yeah, we've had it a while.'

They stared at the clock, and at the angels which appeared to be sleeping. There was so much that was weird about this house, Nick thought, it was no wonder that Gawain could pick things up. It was as if he was wired differently to the rest of them. He grabbed a handful of biscuits as another thought hit him.

'Is your Uncle Kitto a real uncle, you know like flesh and blood real?'

Gawain shook his head, 'No, I was adopted, well sort of adopted, it was all a bit strange. I think I was more – given to Uncle Kitto. He always goes on about me being a … ' he paused.

'A responsibility? My mum always calls me a liability,' Nick said.

Gawain grinned, 'Does she? Can't think why!'

'Thanks!'

'No, with Uncle Kitto it's like… like he's doing a job for someone else. He's always been super-conscientious, almost as if he's following instructions in a manual.'

'What, like making a piece of flat-pack furniture?'

Gawain smiled ruefully, 'Yeah, pretty much.'

'Perhaps more parents should do that,' Nick said thinking about his dad who, more often than not, forgot when he was supposed to be having a day with him.

'Maybe, but it doesn't always mean he gets it right.'

'Why, what's he done?' Nick asked, intrigued.

'Nothing major, but he can sort of pick things up that people are about to do. Remember when you guys came into the shop the first time and he gave Tamar that mug for her mum before she'd even said she wanted it?'

Nick nodded.

'Well, it can put people off. Some of my friends can't cope with it, so they stop coming round. Until you guys came on the scene I was a bit of a Billy no-mates.'

Nick was about to respond when they heard voices coming up the stairs, and one of them was Michael's.

. . .

Servo, the Watcher sat at the back of a café in Pendrym. It was perfectly situated opposite Kitto Cornish's shop. He'd followed Gawain and Nick as they made their way back from Pendrym promenade, and their confrontation with their enemies, and seen them arrive safely at Gawain's home.

Looking out of the window at the crowded street, he'd witnessed Michael appear and glance in the café, and Watched as Michael had swept the street for evidence of the Crow Man and his allies before ducking and entering the little gift shop. If he was meeting with Kitto Cornish something significant had happened.

The waitress came to clear his table and looked at him curiously, 'Have you finished, Sir?'

The Watcher glanced down at his cup. He hadn't touched it. In his Watching he had forgotten the most elementary instruction about how important it was to blend in if one had to mingle with the human race. He was slipping up.

'Mais non, mademoiselle,' he started.

He caught himself. Now he was speaking in the wrong language! If he wasn't careful they'd be sending him on a course again. He shuddered at the thought of the last one; those rows of desks and their lecturer droning on about time-lapse travelling and the art of fitting in. Most of the Watchers had slipped away before the lecture finished, a month-long lesson was more than anyone should have to endure.

The waitress was looking puzzled.

'No, thank you very much,' Servo said. 'I like my coffee cool.'

The waitress looked unconvinced, but to his relief she moved on to the next table. He would have to be more careful.

The Watcher looked out of the window again, stirred his coffee and Watched as a dark figure, coat collar turned up and broad-brimmed hat pulled low over his eyes, walked past the café door.

. . .

Michael strode over to the bay window in Kitto's sitting room above the shop, and looked down to the street below and then to the roof opposite. He knew that their enemies were close by even if they weren't immediately visible.

Then he turned around and looked at the two boys and Kitto Cornish, all waiting expectantly to hear what he had to say, however their old friend just continued to question them.

'So,' he said, 'John Oliver took Arthur back.'

Nick and Gawain nodded.

They watched him pace the room, deep in thought. He glanced at the clock, with the now awake angels, and at the piles of books.

He turned to Gawain's uncle asking, 'Arthur 'as been given the book?'

Kitto Cornish said, 'Yes Michael, he'd opened it and he'd travelled.'

Both men were quiet.

Michael looked at the boys, 'And Tamar 'ad delivered the scroll to him?'

'Yes, we – she gave it to him at Dywana's cottage. He put it somewhere safe, I think, 'cause it was just then that the Crow Man turned up on the beach,' Nick said. As he finished explaining he remembered that they hadn't mentioned the scroll to anyone.

Michael and Kitto exchanged looks.

Then Michael asked, 'An' Tamar?'

'She's at Porth Pyra,' Gawain started. 'Her sister wouldn't let her come over. She had to help in the shop.'

'Have you 'eard from her?' Michael asked them.

'No,' Nick replied, 'but she'll be in the shop till it closes so we wouldn't.'

Michael stopped pacing and became very still and looked at the ceiling, and Nick was taken back to that moonlit night on the moors when they'd been searching for Arthur. Michael had done that then. It was as if he was tuned into something – or somewhere – else.

Kitto said, 'Can you find her?'

Michael shook his head, 'No Kitto, she's hidden from me.'

Gawain and Nick glanced at each other.

'What do you mean?' Nick asked.

But Michael didn't answer his question; once more he looked up at the ceiling and concentrated. After several minutes he nodded and glanced around the room, and then looked at the boys.

'You must take care,' he said to them. 'Just 'cause they've failed this time doesn't mean they'll fail again.'

'The Crow Man and the Pale Guy?' Nick asked. 'I thought they were after Arthur, not us.'

'You're Guardians too, remember, an' as such you're valuable. Don't be thinkin' that you don't count. They know that you 'ave work to do and they will do *anything* to stop you.'

It hadn't occurred to either Nick or Gawain that they held any value because, after all, it was Arthur who'd been made the main Guardian.

'You'll be safe in 'ere,' Michael said, indicating the cottage. 'However, the minute you're outside that door…'

Then he turned to Nick, 'The stone dragon, you've still got it?'

Nick nodded and frowned because, apart from his friends, he didn't think that anyone else knew anything about it. He hadn't even mentioned it to Kitto Cornish, although he'd meant to.

'Hold it up, boy.'

Nick delved into his pocket and pulled out the little statue, showering the floor with the contents of his pocket.

Michael took it and cradled it and turned it round, examining it from every angle.

'Ah, t'is as I thought - Malachite from King Solomon's mines.' He continued, 'Now, if you be from there… and of that time,' he said, talking to the model dragon, 'ow did you get here my friend?'

He peered at it, 'Ah, he's waking.'

Michael held the dragon so that they had a clear view of the statue. As they watched, its tail started to twitch. Then it yawned, and a tiny tongue of flame escaped.

Michael chuckled, 'Now 'ow many years 'ave you been sleepin'?'

He held it out for Nick, 'He's some learnin' to do, 'cause he's only a young 'un.'

Gawain and Nick exchanged glances. A carved dragon coming to life was pushing the boundaries, even for them. Michael, observing their reactions, chuckled once again.

'It's a bit of a shock isn't it?'

The friends nodded mutely, their eyes glued to the antics of the tiny creature. It was stretching its wings and as they watched, it flapped them once as if it was making sure they still worked after so many years, and then it took off. Joyfully it soared above their heads, zigzagging from one side of the room to the other before shooting up to land on the ceiling light. It perched on the lampshade for a moment, took off again and came spiralling down, shot over the back of the armchair, and landed on Nick's shoulder. For a stone dragon with very little flying experience, it seemed remarkably agile.

But Nick was petrified and stood as if he was the one carved from stone. If Gawain hadn't been so amazed by what he'd just witnessed, he would have revelled in the horror written across Nick's face.

Michael was talking to Kitto. 'He knows 'is master,' he said, as if nothing unusual had taken place.

Kitto replied, 'Remarkable! Never in my life did I think that I would witness this. What a joy!'

Joy was not Nick's emotion. Terror would have been a better description.

Michael chuckled once again, crossed the room, slapped Nick once on the back and said, 'He won't need much feedin', an' he'll look after you. When they're this age they mostly eat insects, once they grow they'll be needin' more – but that won't be for a while yet.'

He picked up a book from one of the piles and, opening it, passed it to the boys.

'I believe you were given a book, Nick. It might 'ave been 'elpful if you had looked at it. Books can 'elp in all sorts of ways.'

Gawain glanced at the page open in front of him.

An illustration of a small green dragon returned his gaze.

Underneath the picture there was a caption, 'The rare Malachite.' Below that, in ornate writing, were instructions on the care of dragons and at the end were the words, 'Dangerous if angered.' Gawain decided that he wouldn't show that to Nick just yet.

Michael turned to Kitto Cornish, 'I've got to be on my way, there's work to be done, but the lads will be safe enough 'ere with you Kitto.'

Mr Cornish positively glowed and almost bowed. But neither Nick nor Gawain noticed because they were very aware of a small dragon testing its newly-found flame throwing skills.

. . .

Tamar woke up and, for a few moments, couldn't remember where she was but the moment she moved hot jabs of pain reminded her. She turned over, opened her eyes and groaned. Her shoulder really hurt. Then it all came flooding back to her like a bad dream: that woman, the boat and her fall.

It was dark in the room, with only the very faintest glow coming from the gap above her head. A sprinkling of stars shone high above in the night sky. Tamar peered into the gloom, however judging from the snores, Hairy Face and his dog seemed to be sleeping. She listened for any sounds from beyond the room, but as far as she could make out no one was around.

She sat up very slowly, protecting her shoulder, and as her eyes adjusted to the dim light she scanned the space. A tiny, round window at head height was the only opening, revealed by the brass plate that had covered it swinging back on its hinges. She wondered if she could be bothered to look but, after a few minutes, she gritted her teeth and pulled herself up.

It wasn't a window - it was a port hole. She should have worked it out. They'd brought her to a ship. Tamar stood looking out at the sea, wondering where the ship was moored, when she realised that she could just make out the outline of land against the night sky. She squinted at the grey silhouette of the hills and relief washed over her. She knew this land, she'd spent so many summer days here that the contours of the hills were almost old friends. The boat wasn't in some far-off waters but lying off the coast of Cornwall, just outside the bay at Porth Talant.

'So, you're awake then.'

There was a metallic clatter and Tamar froze.

Hairy face had shuffled to his feet and was standing behind her. From the smell she guessed that he wasn't a great one for baths.

'T'is beautiful by night,' he continued, 'but t'is the fairest of places by sun or moon. They might try to hurt its people but they'll not succeed. Kernow and its folk are strong.'

Tamar was quiet. This wasn't the sort of conversation she would expect from Hairy Face.

She heard clanking and more shuffling as he sat down again. When she was sure he was safely on the other side of the room, she turned around and looked at him. Now that her head was a bit clearer she could see that he was unlikely to be a threat. The beard was a bit overgrown and he could definitely do with a wash but, judging by his eyes, he wouldn't do anyone any harm.

'Who are they?' she asked, referring to her kidnappers.

Hairy Face smiled, revealing a dentist's nightmare. Brushing his teeth was obviously not a high priority either.

'Going to talk to me now? That's good,' he said. 'They are nothing short of evil folk who want to do others harm.'

'Who's the woman?' Tamar asked, the creeping frost etched on her memory.

'The woman? She's the worst of the lot. She gets the others dancin' to her tune. They might seem big and strong and terrible, but she's more evil than the rest put together. She calls 'erself 'The Lady of Clehy''.

'Clehy? '

'Ice.'

'Oh,' said Tamar, shuddering.

'*And* she calls 'erself the True Queen of Kernow, although she ain't. She be no more a queen than I be a king! Her rightful name is the Lady of Darkness.'

He carried on, 'She's been plottin' and planning. The things she's said - it's enough to turn your blood to ice!

T'is worse than when she touches you – and that's bad enough.'

He shivered; he'd obviously had Tamar's experience.

'She reckons she's goin' to rule the whole of Kernow. So that means getting rid of those who would stand in her way. The rightfully appointed Guardians.'

A noise above them, footsteps across what Tamar now knew to be the deck, stopped Hairy Face. They both looked towards the space wondering who would appear, when a spotty face peered down at them.

'S'pose you're hungry,' it said.

Hairy Face said, 'Now lad, we don't need to go through the same routine every morning. Course we're hungry! Just go and find us somethin' and don't forget the dog this time.'

The boy turned away but he was called back, 'And this lass deserves the best that you can offer. None of that stale bread that you're so keen on offerin' me. She's a true Guardian – not a made-up one.'

The spotty face looked at Tamar with a mixture of fascination and awe. Then he collected himself, 'You say she's a Guardian but *you* would. She's only a girl. There's nothing special about her!'

Even though she was feeling sore and her shoulder was agony, Tamar found herself trying to come up with a suitable answer but she was beaten to it by Hairy Face.

'Special or not m' lad, she needs food. Your mistress hurt her, and you know what happens to them who hurts a Guardian!'

Fear flitted across the boy's face.

He said, 'She doesn't look like a Guardian to me. They're meant to be strong – to be able to protect

Kernow, she couldn't even protect herself! If she 'ad special powers or somethin' she'd 'ave got herself out of here. I'll get her somethin' to eat, but not 'cause she's special.'

Hairy Face growled, 'Enough of your arguing - just do as I say boy!'

The boy took a step back as if he'd been hit. Hairy Face hadn't moved, he'd only spoken, but with such authority that no one in their right mind would dare to disobey him. Spotty Face mumbled something and immediately disappeared.

Hairy Face sighed and said, 'He's not a bad lad – just stupid. Ready to follow the first one that offers him a little power.'

Tamar thought about the conversation. How had he known that she was a Guardian? She hadn't breathed a word of it. Hairy face watched her.

'Never mind 'ow I know lass, I know, that's enough for now. When you've eaten I'll tell our young friend to take you and get your shoulder bound up. That should make you a little more comfortable.'

Their conversation was interrupted by a whirring sound which appeared to be coming from Hairy Face's beard. She watched as he reached through the hair and drew something out that glinted and shone. It was about the size of a large coin, but fatter. He pressed it and it sprang open. Light flooded from it, filling the cabin and then Tamar heard chimes like a clock – a very big clock - chiming. They sounded as though they were far off, in another room, or time, but she realised that they were coming from the tiny object held by Hairy Face.

Chapter 13

~ Stone Angel ~

Porth Talant

The phone rang and Arthur heard Dywana go downstairs and pick it up. It was still dark with just a hint of the earliest glimmers of light threading their way beneath his curtains. He was awake anyway. His head had been too full of that picture - and the deep listening to allow him a complete night's sleep. There was a muffled one-way conversation followed by her footsteps coming back up the stairs.

He heard her stop outside his door and then knock hesitantly, before poking her head in and asking, 'Can I come in?'

'Course,' he said, sitting up, but seeing the look on Dywana's face his stomach churned. 'What's wrong, is it Mum or Dad?'

'No,' she said, 'they're fine - it's Tamar.'

'Tamar?'

'Yes,' Dywana paused. 'She's disappeared.'

'Disappeared?'

Dywana nodded, 'That was Morwenna on the phone. They've got all of Porth Pyra out looking for her.'

'When did she go missing? Why didn't Wenna phone before?' Arthur asked.

'She spoke to Gawain and he said that none of you had seen her,' Dywana said. 'But she was hoping that for some reason Tamar might have come here. She disappeared late yesterday afternoon – from the shop. Morwenna went to get her an' lock up, but it was open and empty. It looked as though Tamar 'ad left in a hurry. Some of the ice-cream trays hadn't been washed an' Tamar's phone was still behind the counter.'

'Someone must have seen her leave,' Arthur exclaimed. 'You can't sneeze in Porth Pyra without the whole village being told!'

'Well, no one has any idea where she's gone. She seems to 'ave vanished into thin air,' Dywana said. 'Have you any idea where she might be?'

'No, none.' But a dark dread was growing.

He noticed that the ship on the windowsill was rocking again, 'We'd better get out and look for her. Maybe she's on the cliff path – perhaps she's fallen and hurt herself.'

Dywana sighed, 'I don't think that would help…' and a shadow passed over her face as she added, 'I've a feeling that Brane is behind this.'

'Brane, you mean the Crow Man? But he was in Pendrym, even he can't be in two places at once!'

'No - but there are others with 'im. There are some who refuse to recognise your birthright Art. An' Tamar is also a Guardian. They believe that you will be weakened without her.'

Lightning sat up in his basket and whined.

'But I've got to do something, I can't just stay here!'

Arthur thought about that afternoon and the power of the Crow Man's silent fury - and of his own capture by Matearnas the previous summer. These people were capable of anything.

'Art, it won't 'elp anyone if you put yourself at risk,' she said. 'You are responsible for many more than just your friends.'

'What! Do you mean that you want me to sacrifice Tamar for a load of people I don't know? There's no way I'm doing that!'

Dywana replied, 'You have no choice Arthur, t'is for Kernow that you were Chosen, t'is for Kernow that you were born. You made a pledge an' it cannot be broken.'

Arthur gazed at his aunt in disbelief and shook his head. 'No way,' he said quietly. 'There's no way I'm doing that.'

Dywana paused before replying, 'You must remember that Tamar was also Chosen. Her destiny was to be a Guardian; she will always be prey to the other side.'

The model sailing ship was rocking violently as it sailed across its imaginary ocean, over invisible waves and through a silent gale. Its sails were full and Arthur heard its timbers creaking. Wherever it was, it was battling against the elements. Dywana regarded it seriously, and they both listened as the wind outside the cottage began to pick up, whistling around the chimney and bending the oak branches above the roof.

But Arthur had made his mind up. 'I may have to look out for all of Cornwall but, as far as I'm concerned, that includes Tamar. There's no way that I'm going to abandon her.'

Dywana looked at him and for the first time she saw a young man, not a boy, and understood that nothing she could say would change his mind. And then it hit her; he'd been granted authority over Cornwall and its people – and that included her. She sighed because she knew that the time had come to allow him to make his own choices, whatever that might mean for him and his safety.

'You must do what you feel to be right Arthur - but remember 'ow valuable you are to *them*!'

She looked as if she was going to add something more, but instead she leant down to stroke Lightning and quietly left the room.

As she closed the door behind her, Arthur swung out of bed because an idea was already taking shape.

He reached for the box and, lifting Kitto Cornish's book out, opened it. He examined the picture he'd been looking at earlier and then exclaimed out loud, he hadn't noticed that before! *Now* it was clear where he had to go, although he couldn't see how that would help Tamar.

. . .

It was still very early in Pendrym, hardly a soul stirred at this time of day. Gawain pulled back the hem of the curtain and gazed at the sky, it was a clear blue and the sun was already spreading its low, morning light across the rooftops.

He knelt on his bed and peered down to the street below him and then checked the roofs and chimneys for any evidence of a crow.

A couple of seagulls screeched to one another but no other bird was visible. And if no other birds were around, it was more than likely that the Crow Man wasn't around either.

Pendrym

Gawain knew he shouldn't go out but how could he stay shut up in the cottage when Tamar was in danger? And she was in danger, he could feel it. It wasn't like last year with Arthur on the moors, he'd known then that he had to go to the Granite House but this time he had no idea where to go, or what to do. All he had was a feeling that it was something to do with the past.

The night before, Morwenna had phoned after Michael had left, asking if they'd heard from Tamar. She'd sounded terrible. And as soon as Nick and Gawain were told about how Tamar had disappeared, even leaving her phone behind, they knew it was bad – and they knew it must be connected with the Crow Man and his allies.

Then Nick had told him about his encounter with the woman in black when he and Tamar had been taken back to Porth Pyra by Jago. He'd described the images she'd projected into his mind and the desolation and despair that had washed over him. He'd also told Gawain about the way she'd watched Tamar.

Looking over the rooftops with his chin resting on his folded arms, Gawain thought about all of this and knew that he had to do something. He reasoned that if he could have some quiet time by himself he might just pick up something that would point to Tamar's location. So, trying to quell the voices warning him not to step outside the shop door, Gawain slipped out. He thought about waking Nick, but he decided that his friend probably needed all the sleep he could get after the night they'd had trying to calm a hyper-active dragon on top of their worry for Tamar.

Gawain rounded the corner at the end of the road and walked up a narrow lane with its cottages crowding in on one another, their mossy roofs topping ancient stone and cob walls. There wasn't space enough to allow a car through because these houses had been built many centuries before, when horses had been ridden. His footsteps echoed on the cobbles and he was abruptly aware of just how vulnerable he was. He looked around nervously, but not in time to see a shadow step back into a doorway.

Gawain continued on to the quay, past the fish-market, and down towards the sea. A few seagulls squawked and cried, rising and falling on the sudden gusts of wind while they waited for the fishing boats to arrive with their free breakfasts. The river was a muddy brown, stirred up by the wind and rain which had arrived so suddenly the night before. Everywhere was deserted. He usually liked it quiet but with every step he took he felt more uneasy, as if something or someone was waiting for him. Perhaps he should get back now, maybe he should have told Nick where he was going, or at least have borrowed the dragon. He leant over the railings bordering the promenade and looked out to sea, trying to concentrate on Tamar, so he didn't hear the steps - or sense the presence behind him.

Servo stepped back into the shadows. He'd had a dilemma - whether to stay and Watch the cottage with the other boy, or to follow and Watch this one, but Kitto could be witness to anything that happened back there. A movement alerted the Watcher and confirmed his worst fears because another figure, dark-coated with a crow flying silently above him, had stepped out of the lane and was strolling unseen towards the boy. The man turned and glanced at the Watcher, and grinned, because the Crow Man knew the Rule. He knew that Servo wasn't permitted to intervene, whatever may happen. He slowly raised his arm, a short wooden plank in his hand, before swinging it down towards Gawain's head. The Watcher winced as he heard the crack on Gawain's skull - and Watched as the boy crumpled and hit the ground.

. . .

Over in Porth Talant, unaware of the danger creeping up on Gawain at that very moment, Arthur closed the front door of the cottage and motioned to Lightning to stay at his side. He cast a quick glance around him, checking for any activity, and walked towards a steep lane bordered by high, stone hedges.

The sun was creeping up, casting long shadows along the ground, and the sea was so calm that barely a ripple disturbed the surface. A sleek shape bobbed up at the water's edge and a pair of large, dark eyes watched the boy and his dog. It monitored their progress towards the lane and then there was a 'plop' as it disappeared as silently as it had arrived.

Arthur, unaware of the seal's scrutiny, catalogued everything that he'd experienced and learnt in the last few days. He was lost in thought as he approached his destination, so he barely noticed the breeze drop as he neared the gate, or the silence as the birdsong hushed.

When he'd re-examined the picture in Kitto's book it had been clear that this was the place it was showing him, and he wondered why he hadn't been able to make it out straightaway. After all, he'd spent hours here every time he stayed with Dywana because it was one of his favourite places, although choosing a graveyard as your retreat would seem odd to a lot of people. But Arthur loved the weather-worn headstones engraved with the memories of people who'd populated the village throughout the centuries.

Their names were like old friends. He knew who had lived into old age and which families had been blessed with many children. He was almost on speaking terms with the wealthy inhabitants, marked out by their ornate statues and carvings. It was probably the closest he would ever get to having rich friends!

Arthur pushed the gate open and Lightning shot past, racing up the path ahead of him.

He climbed the steep, slate steps past the empty church and carried on, up to the graveyard on the cliff edge, but Lightning had disappeared.

'Oh no, not again!' he groaned. 'Lightning! Here boy.'

'He's 'ere Arthur, you're alright.'

Arthur spun around.

Sitting on a stone bench with his back to the church wall, was Michael, with Fly and Lightning spinning around one another in giddy circles at his feet.

''ere boy,' Michael said to his dog. 'Calm down!'

'Michael!'

The man looked at Arthur, 'You weren't expectin' me then?'

Arthur shook his head, lost for words. Nothing in the book had indicated that anyone else would be here.

'I wasn't in the picture?'

Again Arthur shook his head.

Michael looked thoughtful, 'Sometimes they books likes to give surprises.'

He paused, 'So then… it hasn't allowed you to see far beyon' the frontispiece, maybe it thinks this is the wisest way.'

Arthur thought about how he'd found the book in Gawain's house. It had been as if it had presented itself to him. As if it had said, 'Ta dah! Here I am, pick me up.' He'd never thought of a book having a mind of its own.

He looked up to see Michael watching him and the colours came flooding into his mind and, before he knew it, he was deep talking with his old friend, exchanging their worries and concerns. It felt as if the last year hadn't happened and they'd never had to say goodbye, it was so much easier than using ordinary words. Eventually he calmed down and the colours faded.

Michael said gravely, 'You've learnt much, Sire. John Oliver has done 'is work well.'

Then he nodded to something behind Arthur, 'But you came 'ere because of the picture.'

There was a sound - a dry scraping, and Arthur turned, wondering what could be behind him. There was nothing, only a graveyard full of tombstones and statues, and then the dogs came and stood either side of him.

But then he saw it; the very merest of movements. He held his breath, certain that he must be seeing things but no - there it was again. Michael came and stood at his side, and put his hand on Arthur's shoulder.

'Sire, he's been waitin' for many years to make your acquaintance. We were goin' to wait for Angela but she 'as other work to do in another place - she'll be sorry to have missed you. Maybe she'll be able to join us all later.'

The stone angel rearranged its wings and lowered its arm, which had been outstretched over the sea.

Then very slowly, and stiffly, he stepped off the plinth and moved towards Arthur. It was only Michael standing beside him that stopped Arthur from sprinting down the path and right away from the graveyard. Even with his old ally beside him he could feel his heart pounding.

Although the angel was moving the expression carved on his face didn't change, adding to the overall effect, and Arthur's fear.

'Sire, may I present my namesake to you? He too is called Michael, although t'is easier to call him Pierre.'

'Pierre?' Arthur echoed, thinking that nothing could have prepared him for this. A walking statue - and one with a name!

'Pierre means rock or stone in French. It's our little joke,' Michael chuckled softly.

'Joke?' Arthur repeated weakly. He'd heard it all now.

'Life can be awful dull without a bit of laughter, we all need it, even in the darkest of times,' Michael said. 'And why should we be the only ones to laugh?'

Arthur glanced at Michael, wondering if he was joking but he clearly meant it. By now the angel was standing in front of Arthur, and it was then that he heard the words. They were gold, liquid gold, and they poured through him, calming and reassuring him, and he looked up into the statue's face and saw that it was attempting to smile. Perhaps it would have been better if it hadn't.

The angel bowed, rather stiffly.

'Pierre 'as his part to play in all of this,' Michael said. 'He has been guardin' this part of Kernow for many, many years. Guardin' it from those who wish it harm.'

Arthur looked at the statue, how could it possibly protect anything?

Michael continued, 'Those wishin' to stir up the land are gathering and their numbers make them more powerful. They've stirred up memories; maybe you've 'eard them.'

The storm and the screams came back to Arthur and he remembered Gawain had said something about feeling as though the past was reaching out. Arthur knew that some seriously bad stuff had happened around here, although you could say that about anywhere, but he thought about the smuggling, the highwaymen and the shipwrecks. Maybe those screams he'd heard in that freak storm had been the screams of people drowned off the shore. He shuddered. Pieces were starting to fall into place.

The angel adjusted its wings and slowly lifted its arm. The hand was set as though it should be holding something. Arthur stared. He knew what was missing.

...

On the little beach below the church and its graveyard, Viatoris had arrived from five hundred years away in Italy and stood looking up at the three figures silhouetted on the cliff. If the angel statue had been woken from its slumber then matters must be moving.

The waves lapped on to the shore. The little boy played, running in and out of the water, squealing every time the water touched his feet. The Watcher glanced at him, making sure he was safe. They were the only two on the beach and Viatoris congratulated himself on his idea. There would be no one else around for a little while yet. No one else to observe him, or the boy, dressed in such unusual clothes.

He'd managed to haul the child with him across the years when he'd felt the first pulls back to this time and place. The child had seemed unbothered but he had a fascinating mind, always ready for new ideas and experiences. The Watcher thought guiltily about the Rule but this was the only time he'd broken it, he was sure that no harm would come of it. There was nothing in this peaceful, secluded bay to speak of this century – no cars or trains. Nothing.

'Aqua!' the boy shrieked.

'Ssshh,' Viatoris said, looking towards the figures on the cliff nervously.

Michael mustn't see them, he would be angry if he knew that the Rule had been ignored. Or maybe not angry, perhaps just disappointed. And it was far worse to feel Michael's disappointment. Perhaps he should take the boy back to his own time before they were seen.

He moved to take the boy's hand but at that moment there was a movement in the sky above them and the boy stood transfixed; watching as a small, single-seater plane flew slowly across the morning sky. Leonardo followed its flight as it travelled from east to west, and Viatoris' heart sank. He understood that by breaking the Rule he'd changed the course of history - and the natural flow of events. The seed had been sown in the brilliant mind of the child. He knew that flight by man was possible.

Viatoris frowned. He'd take the boy back straightaway before he had a chance to see anything else. He held the boy's hand and there was a crackle and a *'woomph'* as the man and boy disappeared.

On the cliff above the beach Michael watched the plane and smiled to himself. The Watcher would have some explaining to do.

Chapter 14

~ The pocket watch ~

In the wooden prison on board the ship, Hairy Face looked towards the ceiling, and the dog stood with its ears pricked.

Shouts carried down to them. He'd wanted to tell the girl more about the pocket watch and its purpose, but that would have to wait. He couldn't risk it falling into their hands.

Hairy Face put his finger to his lips, lifted his beard and secreted the silver disc beneath it. Hearing the voices, Tamar swallowed all the questions that she was desperate to ask. Whatever her fellow prisoner had been holding, it was something out of this world. She'd felt drawn towards it and a dizziness, a strangely similar sensation to being pulled back in time by Zephaniah, but her attention was diverted by the conversation on the deck above them.

The woman was saying, 'I told you not to harm him! He was by himself, he would have been no match for you.'

'We couldn't risk allowing him to escape again,' a man's voice was replying. 'And look at the girl! Her injuries at *your* hands still trouble her.'

'They are nothing in comparison to your clumsy handling of the boy. He may not live!' She was shouting now.

But the man sounded unruffled by her anger, 'Is that my concern?'

'Brane, it will not further our cause if you murder our opponents. That is not the way to power. You will only succeed in making them more powerful because many are on their side.'

'It is the way to avenge *her* death though,' the man continued, and now Tamar knew who was speaking. It was the Crow Man and he wanted justice for Matearnas' death. And immediately Tamar was transported to that night on the moors when Matearnas had made her final decision and thrown herself off that ledge. Even now she could see the body falling through the air to land, broken, on the rocks far below.

A brief silence greeted this statement before the man continued, 'And now we have two of them, so we have halved their power. They need to be together in order to achieve their goal. Now that cannot be accomplished.'

Tamar was chilled by the indifference in his voice. If ever he'd had normal, human emotions, they were long gone.

But the argument was interrupted.

Another voice was asking a question, 'Where shall I put him, Ma'am? Do you wish him to be put with the others?'

'Of course,' the woman said impatiently. 'There is nowhere else!'

Something was being hauled across the deck above them. Tamar looked up because whatever was being dragged over the boards was about to be dropped into their space. A body, inert and limp, lay at the edge of the hole.

It was Gawain.

'No!' Tamar shouted.

A face peered down at her; it was the Crow Man. He smiled and, very carefully and deliberately, put his foot in the small of Gawain's back and pushed, all the time watching for her reaction.

Gawain's lifeless body tumbled towards the hard, wooden floor but Hairy Face was positioning himself under the hatch in order to break his fall. Tamar watched helplessly as her friend's body crashed into the little man, and Hairy Face collapsed under the dead weight. The Crow Man looked down but his smile faded when he realised that Gawain's fall had been broken, and that his plan to cause even more harm had been thwarted. He turned away, disgusted.

However it was clear that the Crow Man had already succeeded in inflicting terrible injuries on Gawain, because fresh blood still trickled from his skull through his matted hair. His clothes were torn, old blood was congealing and darkening on his t-shirt and jeans, and he was deathly white.

. . .

In the graveyard above Porth Talant bay, Arthur sat beside his old friend with their dogs at his feet. It was fortunate that he was unaware of the drama taking place on the ship moored behind Lemayne Island. As he looked out to sea, he listened to Michael's instructions.

'So I have to do that by myself?'

Michael nodded, 'The last part, yes.'

'Will there be others waiting?'

Again Michael nodded.

Arthur asked, 'Will any of them be on our side?'

'Some will - but not all.'

Arthur watched a tiny single-seater plane quietly cross the sky, the faint drone of its engine weaving its way to the ground below, everything looked so peaceful, so perfect.

He glanced down as a movement on the beach caught his eye, but whatever had been there had disappeared.

Then he turned his attention back to the angel and said, with more confidence than he felt, 'I'll bring it back, Pierre.'

The statue looked at him impassively, (it was the only way it could look) and spoke deep words.

Arthur listened and nodded, 'I know, I'll do my best. I'll let you know how I'm getting on.'

He turned to Michael, 'When should I go?'

'You'll know the right time; it will be shown to you.'

Then Michael looked at the sky and listened, Arthur knew not to interrupt him but he saw a shadow pass across his face. Michael's eyes seemed to be focused somewhere else, as if he could see beyond the visible world, and then he regarded the angel seriously and spoke deep words. However they were so carefully controlled that Arthur couldn't even begin to guess at them, but he knew that something was wrong. Very wrong.

Michael gathered himself, 'Sire, whatever 'appens you must not be distracted from your goal. Cornwall's fate lies in your 'ands.'

There was a rasping sound as the statue started to move back towards its plinth.

'What's happened?' Arthur asked. 'Is it Tamar, has she been hurt?'

'Tamar is beyond my reach,' Michael said. 'I cannot hear 'ow she is, nor where she is.'

'Who is it then?'

But Michael ignored Arthur's question saying, 'Sire, remember what I said; you must not be diverted from the course set for you. No one else can fill your shoes.'

Their meeting was being brought to a close. Arthur knew Michael well enough to understand when his questions wouldn't be answered, but a part of him also knew that someone close to him was in real danger.

Michael called to his dog and laid his hand on Arthur's shoulder. He gestured to the statue, now back in its place looking out to sea with its arm held high and said, 'Remember that all you do is for Cornwall, for Kernow, an' the many in your care - Sire.'

Then he was on his way, striding down the path, with Fly at his side.

Arthur watched him go with a sinking heart. He didn't know what lay ahead of him, but he had a feeling that it was going to be far more dangerous than merely being kidnapped by Matearnas.

A helicopter buzzed into view, one of the rescue helicopters used when people were in trouble or went missing. Arthur watched it flying low over the sea and itched to do something useful to find Tamar, but he was learning to listen. He had to wait until he was told exactly where he had to go. He sighed and turned, retracing his steps to the cottage.

...

Out at sea the ship rolled, catching the waves that rose and swelled beneath her.

In the door-less prison beneath the deck, Tamar and her companion were silent, shocked by the appearance of the boy who had been thrown down from the deck above them. Hairy Face carefully eased his arms from under Gawain's inert form, laying the boy gently on the cabin's boards, before struggling to his feet. Gawain remained motionless and silent, the scarcely perceptible rise and fall of his chest the only clue that he was still alive – that and the ribbon of blood trickling from his head.

But the dog was already on her feet, ready to administer her own, unique brand of first aid as Hairy Face commanded, 'Sit, hound!'

And there was such fury in those two, short words that the dog immediately sat.

Hairy Face looked down at Gawain, ''Ow dare they do this! They will pay for it. First the girl and then this, they b'aint be fit to rule any land.'

Gawain groaned.

Tamar asked Hairy Face, 'Is he going to be alright?'

He looked up from studying Gawain's injuries and seemed to be considering his reply. Tamar's heart thudded.

'I'm no doctor, miss. I cannot give you an answer.'

She gazed at Gawain and then she shouted to their captors, 'You can't leave him like this!'

But everyone had disappeared.

She'd never felt so helpless, but then her eyes settled on a pile of old, grey sacks in the corner and she remembered that she'd been told that if someone was injured or in shock they should be kept warm. That was something she could do anyway. Quickly, she mobilised Hairy Face and together they found the least dirty and dusty sacks and dragged them over to cover Gawain. Tamar tucked them in and around him as best she could and sat down beside him, watching over him, determined to protect him from any further harm. She sat with her hand on his arm, and talked quietly to him, just as Arthur had done with Lightning. If it had worked for him maybe it could work for her.

'P'raps he's best left for a while, lass,' Hairy Face said gently. "is breathin' is a little stronger.'

Tamar studied Gawain. Was it her imagination or was his breathing deeper? She examined his face, hardly daring to believe it, but she was sure that his colour was returning. She breathed out, daring to hope that maybe he was going to be alright - despite the Crow Man's best efforts to the contrary.

Hairy Face looked up at the hatch, as if he was checking that no one was around, before shuffling across the cabin and settling down beside her.

'Look lass,' he instructed. 'I knows that you're worried 'bout your friend but there's something here that may 'elp him.'

Then delving beneath the black, wiry beard that wound its way over his chest, he drew out the object that he'd hidden there. Now she could see it clearly; it was a pocket watch. It wasn't chiming but she could hear the mechanism whirring as, very carefully, he held it out to her. It was the most beautiful object she'd ever seen. On one side the case was inlaid with tiny, green jewels and on the other it was elaborately engraved silver.

'Go on lass, take it.'

She reached out to touch it and the ticking amplified.

Hairy Face chuckled despite their companion's state, 'I've found its rightful owner then.'

Tamar examined the tiny clock and opened it. Roman numerals marked the time but in the centre of the face, framed by the numbers, was a picture.

She held it close and saw that a man dressed in a frock coat was painted standing outside a cottage. It was Zephaniah – she'd know that moustache anywhere! She marvelled at the artist who could paint in miniature with that much accuracy, but as she inspected the picture Zephaniah waved. Not only did he wave but he turned and walked away, right out of the clock.

Tamar nearly dropped it.

The light coming from the watch died away, but its ticking continued contentedly in the presence of its new, young owner. They'd be going places together.

Tamar was speechless. She turned the pocket watch over as if she might find Zephaniah on the other side, but he'd gone.

'How did it do that? Is it some sort of special effect? That was Zephaniah wasn't it? I met him the other day.'

She was burbling, 'Perhaps it happens if you look at it in a certain light. I've seen 3D pictures but they're not as good as that.'

'Hold it near your friend, lass,' Hairy Face said, ignoring her ramblings. 'Near 'is ear.'

Tamar wondered what this could do for Gawain, but did as she was instructed. Music drifted out towards her, it was very faint, and she thought that she heard a voice. Gawain shifted, moaning, as if he was responding to the music or words. She looked questioningly at Hairy Face but he didn't say a word, just smiled that gap-toothed smile. However at that very moment footsteps echoed along the deck above them and Hairy Face hurriedly grabbed the pocket watch from Tamar's hand, snapped it shut, and replaced it under his beard.

'Not a word, lass,' he whispered. 'We don't want it fallin' into the wrong 'ands!'

Tamar didn't need to be told, although she longed to find out what Hairy Face had meant about finding its rightful owner, but now a face had appeared at the hatch above them.

Chapter 15

~ Nick's challenge ~

'And so now,' the reporter was saying, 'it appears that there are two missing young people. The police are investigating, and both the Coastguard service and Air-Sea Rescue helicopters are scouring the sea off the Cornish shore.'

Nick and Arthur sat glued to the television in Dywana's sitting room, while the tiny, green dragon perched on Nick's shoulder. It was fascinated by the moving images on the screen and from time to time it would dart forwards in an effort to catch something that caught its eye. But Arthur was so distracted by his friends' disappearance that even a small, flying dragon couldn't divert his attention. After all he'd just had his own experience of stone statues coming to life - although this one was definitely more appealing.

. . .

The morning had started badly for Nick. He'd been woken by a miniature dragon landing on his face before it had propelled itself towards the ceiling, made a soaring circuit of the room and snapped up a small fly.

That wasn't so bad. In fact Nick had realised that he was rather pleased to have a dragon as a companion but, as he lay in bed following its flight, Tamar's disappearance had come flooding back to him. He'd turned towards Gawain's bed only to realise that it was empty, and that was the point when the morning had taken a serious turn for the worse.

Desperate to talk to his friend about all that had happened the previous day, he'd called to his dragon and made his way to the kitchen only to discover that Gawain wasn't there; or anywhere else in the cottage. He'd gone down to the shop to ask Mr Cornish where Gawain was, just as the door had been flung open by a red-faced local man.

'Here,' the man had started, breathing heavily, 'Kitto, there's a plank been found near the harbour, an' it's covered in blood!'

And instantly Nick had known that it must be Gawain's blood.

At precisely that moment John Oliver had arrived. He'd glanced at the dragon, now curled up on Nick's shoulder, ushered the local man outside and turned the sign in the shop doorway from 'open' to 'closed'.

'Come on Kitto, let's go up to your sittin' room.'

Nick had followed and listened as John Oliver had tried to calm Gawain's uncle.

Kitto Cornish had been beside himself, shaking his head and muttering, 'I should have taken more care, the boy was entrusted to me.'

'Listen Kitto,' John Oliver said, 'none of this is your doin'. You 'ad no idea he'd gone.'

They'd pushed the embroidered curtain aside and entered the cluttered sitting room. There'd been a chill in the air and, although there was nothing to see, Nick was certain that he could detect a sense of restlessness from among the books. Furthermore, the angels in the grandfather clock had disappeared - and the fire had gone out. In all the time Nick had known Gawain the fire had *never* gone out. There were still embers burning, but only just.

John Oliver had continued to speak to Mr Cornish in hurried, hushed tones, calming him as best he could but also putting forward what had to be done. Nick couldn't hear much, but he was fairly certain that it included him. Then John Oliver had offered to take Nick around to Porth Talant.

'I'll come back 'ere Kitto, but this lad 'as to be with Arthur. He 'as work to do.'

He'd rested his hand on Mr Cornish's shoulder, reassuring him, and said, 'We'll get Gawain home again, Kitto. Their power might seem strong but we know that the foundations are rotten. T'is nothin' against the Power we work for.' Then he'd urged Mr Cornish to stay in the cottage, and hurried Nick down to the harbour and into the boat.

Neither of them had spoken on the short journey from Pendrym to Porth Talant. John Oliver had been on constant alert, scouring the hills and cliffs for any further threat, while Nick had been kept extremely busy trying to prevent a curious dragon from escaping from his pocket.

A figure had been on the beach at Porth Talant, waiting for them. Once again Dywana had been ready.

...

Nick's thoughts were interrupted by the television displaying a picture of Tremelin's ice-cream shop, where Tamar had been working before she'd disappeared.

'Both young people are thought to be close friends, so one line of thought is that they may be together,' the reporter said.

Photos of Tamar and Gawain flashed up on to the screen before returning to the reporter standing in front of the shop.

'There are no clues as to how they disappeared and there are no witnesses to either of them vanishing. In fact it appears that Tamar Tamblyn did exactly that – vanish. As far as we can tell she was in the shop until nearly five o'clock. We have witnesses up until that time but after that there were no further sightings. So please, if you see either of these youngsters, call this number.'

The programme continued in the studio with two presenters sitting behind desks looking suitably concerned, but very quickly it had moved on to a piece about organic vegetables.

Arthur punched the control and threw it across the room.

'How can they talk about carrots and potatoes when Gawain and Tamar have been kidnapped!' he shouted. 'It's mad!'

And then he was on his feet, gesturing out of the window at the people congregated on the beach. 'Look at them, I bet they don't care about organic veg!'

A helicopter buzzed over the cottage, part of the search that the reporter had been describing. Boats criss-crossed the bay, while on the beach the usually, happy family scene, had been replaced by groups being organised into search parties. Any children were being kept very close to their parents.

'No one's going to find them are they?' Nick said, referring to the search taking place all around them. 'There's no way that they'll be somewhere obvious. The Crow Man will see to that.'

'Why on earth did Gawain go out by himself?' Arthur asked. 'He *knew* they were around.'

'I don't know,' Nick replied. 'It's not like him. He didn't say anything the night before and we knew then that Tamar was missing.'

A thought struck Arthur, 'D'you think that Gawain had any idea where she was - like when he knew I was going to the Granite House?'

Nick shook his head.

'He didn't say anything to me but to be honest we'd been kept pretty busy with him,' he said, gesturing towards the dragon which was now inspecting the log basket.

They subsided into silence. Lightning looked from one to the other and then at the dragon. He stood up and whined and Nick was transported back to the previous summer, when the dog had appeared outside the café and escorted them to the train station before the Crow Man could catch them.

Arthur looked at him. 'What is it boy? I can't take you out for a walk now!'

The dog went over to the door and sniffed along the floor to be met with a scratching from the other side. Arthur opened it and the cat strode in with its tail held high. It glanced towards the tiny dragon, now on Nick's shoulder, and then it jumped onto the windowsill and looked out.

Arranged along the previously empty beach wall was the cat's feline defence force. Once again they'd turned up in huge numbers – and once again it appeared that most people didn't see them. Arthur had a brief recollection of last summer when the cats had arrived outside his house. Exactly the same thing had happened then. Somehow they were able to make themselves invisible to everyone - except those who were meant to see them.

Satisfied that it had made its point, the cat jumped off the window sill, prowled over to Arthur and brushed against his legs. Suddenly the boys didn't feel so alone and for the first time that day Arthur felt an idea take hold.

'Let's see if the book will open any further,' he said.

'What, Mr Cornish's book?' Nick asked.

Arthur nodded, 'It may give us an idea; it's worth a try anyway.'

Seizing this possibility they ran up the stairs followed by Lightning and a tiny, flying dragon while, in the kitchen, the knight in the painting sat on his horse and listened. Arthur flung his door open, seized the end of the bed and dragged it away from the wall revealing a tiny door. Grabbing the door's handle he yanked it open, leaned in to the space behind it and pulled out his box.

'I never knew that was there,' Nick said.

'That's the idea,' Arthur replied. 'Only Dywana knows about it... and now you, of course.'

The box lid sprang off as if it had been waiting for Arthur to get to it, and he reached in and pulled out the yellowed scroll followed by the book given to him by Mr Cornish. The book flipped open of its own accord, choosing the page it wanted Arthur to see.

Arthur and Nick gazed at the drawing in front of them. There was no doubt that the book wanted them to see this page, it wouldn't let them open it anywhere else. The ship on the windowsill had stilled and downstairs the knight in the painting smiled, but out at sea a storm cloud grew.

'So, do you think we have to go there?' Nick asked.

Arthur considered the picture on the scroll and in the book.

'I have to go there, but I think you're meant to be around here,' he said. 'Michael told me that I have to do that bit by myself.'

'What can I do here? Wouldn't it be better if we went together?'

Arthur shook his head, 'I wish we could but Michael was really clear about it. And you know how he is when he gives you advice.'

Nick sank into a thoughtful silence. There was no way he'd ignore Michael's directions either. 'Oh, okay then, but I wish I could come too.'

'Me too, mate! Believe me this wouldn't be my choice of a fun evening out.'

Arthur turned to studying the picture on the scroll and Nick peered over his shoulder. It was a map but now it was coming to life, becoming a living map. Even as they looked at it they could see the grass moving, and the water rippling. A bird soared above the tor in the background and the clouds billowed, blown by the silent wind.

'Man, that's something else!' Nick said, watching the picture.

'Yeah, it's cool isn't it?'

Nick nodded mutely and then a thought struck him, 'Look mate, if you really do have to go by yourself, how about taking the dragon?'

But Arthur quickly refused this offer as well, 'No, I think you're going to need him.' He glanced over to see the tiny creature making himself comfortable on his friend's shoulder. 'And anyway, I don't think he'd leave you.'

He looked back to the scroll, the words were becoming clearer. Two lines leapt out at him and a couple of other words were revealing themselves.

'From water she comes,
a sword in her hand.
The bearer's.........'

He glanced from the scroll back to the book and more pieces of the puzzle slotted into place. He was going to have to ask his friend to do something he wouldn't wish on his worst enemy, but there was no one else left. Gawain and Tamar needed any protection he could offer - and that involved Nick.

'Listen,' Arthur started. 'I'm going to have to ask you to do something... ' he trailed off.

Words and phrases jangled about protecting Cornwall and her people, yet here he was about to ask Nick to put himself in real danger.

...

High above the cottage, the Watchers stood together on the cliff top looking out to sea.

A tall-masted ship floated across the water with its sails billowing even though there wasn't even a hint of a breeze.

On the beach below them the Writer sat on a rock. She glanced up at the helicopter above her, buzzing the cliffs before banking out to sea and back again, and listened to the radio conversation relayed between the pilot and his crew. She watched as boats of all shapes and sizes swarmed on the sea, their crews determined to do anything they could to help to find Tamar and Gawain. Everyone had pulled together in an effort to find the missing youngsters but no one took any notice of the sailing ship, powered by a non-existent wind.

A voice knocked on her thoughts, interrupting her listening to the conversation in the helicopter.

'The stone angel has woken, Ma'am. He has spoken with the Chosen One.' It was Viatoris, one of the Watchers.

The Writer nodded.

'And two of the four have been taken.'

Again the Writer nodded. She knew all of this.

'But Ma'am, surely something must be done!' the Watcher's voice protested. 'The boy's life hangs in the balance, he is holding on by a thread.'

The Writer frowned; the Watchers knew the Rule.

On the cliff high above her Viatoris put his hand to his head. When the Writer was displeased she made it very clear - and her reply had been so sharp that it had actually stung. Servo looked at his companion and sympathised because he'd suffered those words, they hurt. A lot.

Together they saw the Writer take out her pen and start to Write. The ink was red. They glanced at one another because red was the worst colour – almost. There was one colour which they dreaded more.

The Writer paused in her writing and looked over to the cottage as Arthur's words floated out to her. She was impressed with how quickly he'd mastered the deep listening and the deep talking, he was already proving himself to be a worthy heir to the title; however there was still the final part of the king-making to be done. Nothing was certain until that had been accomplished.

She sighed silently and buried her deepest thoughts. She too wished that the Rule could be broken but it was vital to maintain the proper order of things, however hard that might be.

Thunder rolled, a storm was brewing.

The paths and beach were emptying as the search parties began to move away along the coast. The sky too was clearing as the helicopter flew above other bays and beaches in an effort to spot anything which might lead them to the teenagers.

Both Watchers observed an open boat appear from the direction of Porth Pyra, powered by a small outboard engine. Slowly the little craft made its way through the, now deserted, waters towards the sailing ship, rolling on the swelling seas. They examined the man steering the boat, then they glanced at one another - and smiled.

They Watched as Jago Jolliff adjusted his boat's course to approach the ship's stern and wondered whether he'd be able to get to the ship without being seen. They knew that his plan would only succeed if he maintained the element of surprise. If anyone on board spotted him any hope of rescue would be lost.

...

In the bedroom of the little cottage, Arthur sat with Kitto's book on his knee and the scroll by his side. As convincingly as possible he'd outlined the situation to Nick, and what he felt had to be done. He wasn't happy about any of it but he had no choice.

'So,' Arthur said, 'you see, you *have* to stay there. If they gain control over it, they've won.'

Nick hadn't said a word throughout Arthur's explanation and at the end he sat in silence. Lightning pushed his muzzle into his hand and Nick stroked the dog while he weighed up what Arthur had asked him to do. Last year when he'd promised that they'd stand together he'd meant every word, but he hadn't imagined them being divided like this.

The Crow Man and his allies had seriously weakened their defence. Now it was just him and Arthur, and they had to work separately.

'It's okay I get it,' Nick said. 'I'll go in a minute. When are you going?'

Arthur glanced at his watch and realised that it was later than he'd thought, 'I'll have to go soon before it gets too dark. I'll probably catch the train.'

'You'd better take my key then, 'cause there won't be anyone at home. Mum's working night shifts so she'll be out before you get there.' Nick took his keys and handed them to Arthur. 'My bike's around the back of the house in the usual place, you'll have to unlock the gate at the side to get to it.'

He ground to a halt and he and Arthur stared at one another. It sounded so strange to be discussing ordinary things like work - and front door keys. Their normal lives seemed a million miles away. As if to emphasise this the dragon yawned and belched, sending a wispy spiral of smoke towards the ceiling, before he nestled into Nick's neck.

Arthur nodded, 'It's probably just as well she won't be there. Can you imagine trying to to explain why I'm borrowing it?'

Nick grinned, 'Umm yes, it might be interesting!'

Downstairs a door opened, footsteps crossed the hall and a door closed.

'What about Dywana?' Nick asked. 'Won't she be worried?'

'We've sort of discussed it already, it's cool.' But even as he was saying this Arthur could hear her deep words seeping into his mind. He replied, trying his best to reassure her, but the problem with the deep talking was that it was almost impossible to hide the words' true meaning.

The dragon flicked its tail. Nick picked it up, holding it away from himself just as a jet of fire shot out of its mouth like a mini flame-thrower.

'Look, try and control it!' he said to the animal. 'Remember, I'm not the enemy.'

Blinking, the dragon licked its burning jaws (throwing fire was an acquired art), and curled up again.

Nick carefully opened his pocket and slipped the creature inside.

'No more fire until I say, okay?'

Despite what lay ahead of them, Arthur grinned. The sight of Nick talking to a miniature, fire-breathing dragon was surreal, even in their strange, new world.

Nick heaved himself out of Arthur's chair and listened as the thunder rumbled in the distance. Stepping over piles of clothes and discarded trainers, he made his way to the door.

He turned to Arthur, 'See you later mate, take care.'

Arthur nodded, 'Yeah, you too. Hey, how about having a barbecue on the beach? We won't need matches now you've got the dragon!'

Nick grinned briefly, 'Yeah, that'll be cool.'

Then his smile disappeared and Arthur added seriously, 'Good luck.'

'You too, mate,' Nick said and, checking the dragon was tucked safely inside his pocket, closed the door behind him.

Chapter 16

~ Dragon and the Watcher ~

ROSIE

Gawain was sitting, propped up against the wall of the cabin. The blood on his face had dried although red, glistening beads still oozed from the open wound on his head. His sight was hazy but he could just make out a small, bearded figure merging with the lengthening shadows.

He knew that Tamar was sitting beside him and he was vaguely aware of something ticking in her hand and her conversation with the stranger, but the words didn't make any sense to him.

'Lass, you must keep it, t'is yours. Zephaniah wanted you to 'ave it,' the man was saying.

'How do you know he wanted me to have it? Did he leave a letter or something?' Tamar asked.

'No lass, t'is what he told me. He said that the one who was the first to arrive would be the one who was to be the Time Keeper.'

Tamar did a quick calculation and then she looked at Hairy Face and frowned. 'But he lived ages ago; he couldn't have said anything to you about a ... Time whatsit!'

'Remember 'ow you met him? We aren't all prisoners of our own century.'

The pocket watch ticked and glowed.

On the lid the words, '*To be kept by the Time Keeper*' were engraved, interlaced with moving pictures. Underneath, in tiny letters, a list of names was inscribed. Tamar studied the names and picked out Zephaniah's, and then she noticed that the list was growing. An invisible hand was scratching a 'T' and then an 'a', her name was being added - Tamar Tamblyn. Beneath the cover the pocket watch adjusted its ticking until its cogs rotated and turned to the rhythm of the beats of the Time Keeper's heart. Pulse and cogs in perfect harmony.

Tamar covered the watch protectively, she was all too aware of their jailers on the deck somewhere above them, and then she thought about her brief meeting with Zephaniah and being whisked from one time to another. What could it mean to be a Time Keeper? While she wondered about this, and the implications of what she'd been told, she saw that something was happening to her companion - Hairy Face was becoming blurred.

She blinked. Not only was he losing definition but he was also becoming transparent, there was even a hint of the wooden panelling of the cabin wall showing through his body.

'Do you know you're sort of... ' she considered her words carefully. 'That you're sort of dissolving.'

'Yes lass, I know t'is startin'. Don't let it worry you. I was hopin' that it wouldn't happen yet, I didn't want you to 'ave to see it.'

Hairy Face smiled a broad, peaceful smile, 'T'is the Callin', but it's not somethin' to worry about, t'is somethin' good.'

Tamar frowned. One minute Hairy Face was talking about time travel and the next he was becoming transparent and saying something about the 'Calling'. Then she thought about Zephaniah walking out of the watch. It could just be that she was going mad - it was probably the most likely explanation. But in the middle of these thoughts another came pushing to the front of the queue.

She took a deep breath and, trying to ignore what was happening in front of her, said, 'If Zephaniah wanted me to have it, why didn't he give it to me when he gave me the scroll?'

Hairy Face grinned, 'He said, you'd be asking me that!'

He chuckled and tried to slap his dissolving leg, 'He always was a clever un was Zephaniah.'

'Well, why didn't he?' she asked. It suddenly felt very important to know the answer.

'He ran out of time. *She* was hot on your heels, 'e told me,' Hairy Face said. 'He said that she was sniffin' you out like a fox with a rabbit.'

Tamar nodded, 'She was.'

She looked hard at Hairy Face. He appeared to be solid again but she had a feeling that he might not stay that way for long. She had so many unanswered questions but footsteps were approaching. They both looked towards the hatch, waiting to see who would appear, and Tamar slipped the watch deep into her pocket, but there was a shout and the steps stopped.

Hairy Face surveyed Tamar, 'You and your friend are goin' to 'ave to get out of here. You're not safe, neither of you.'

'There's no way we can get out, look at Gawain, he can only just sit up,' Tamar protested. 'And there's loads more I still need to know!'

'Well, e's going to 'ave to move, lass,' Hairy Face said. 'An' your questions will find answers, but not now.'

Tamar looked up at the hatch, high in the ceiling above them and at Gawain, pale and barely conscious, and her heart sank. She didn't see how they could escape.

Footsteps again. This time they brought their owner to the edge of the hatch, it was the spotty boy.

Hairy Face called up to him, 'Now lad, 'ow about lettin' us up for a breath of air. T'is hot as an oven down 'ere. An' we're not goin' anywhere.'

Spotty Face looked down at them, 'No way! It's more than my life's worth. They'll be mad if you come up 'ere.'

He looked at Hairy Face and assumed what he probably thought was a cunning expression.

'I bet that you're goin' to tell me some daft tale about him bein' a Guardian too,' he said, sneering.

'Well,' started Hairy Face, 'I wasn't goin' to tell you but as you said it… ' And he let his words trail away.

Doubts flashed up, illuminating the worries that the boy had dismissed to the furthest corners of his mind. He glanced from Gawain to Tamar who returned his look with what she hoped was a challenging glare. She needn't have worried, her look was more powerful than she realised. Hairy Face watched the interchange with interest. This girl had more power in her little finger than the boy would ever have.

The boy's confidence melted under the heat of Tamar's stare. What if they really were Guardians and he'd allied himself with the wrong side?

He shuffled uncomfortably and glanced around. His masters had gone below, he could hear them talking and the occasional clink of glasses. They were eating and drinking so he'd be safe for a while, maybe he'd allow the prisoners up – surely it couldn't do any harm? Hairy Face and Tamar watched the thoughts flit across the boy's face and waited.

'Oh, alright then, I'll get the ladder,' he offered reluctantly. 'Just for a couple of minutes an' then straight back down. No funny business or you'll be for it. I've got a pistol 'ere.'

Tamar said, 'Do we look like we could do anything? Your bosses have done a good enough job of making sure we can't go anywhere!'

But all the time she was talking, another part of her brain was busy wondering how they could escape – and how she could get Gawain up the rickety ladder that the boy was positioning at the edge of the hatch.

She turned to Hairy Face, 'Are you coming?'

He shook his head and pointed to the shackles around his ankles.

'No lass, I'm stayin' here. The dog and I will be fine where we are.'

'But you can't..' Tamar started urgently under her breath. 'If you stay here and we get out, they'll know you helped us.'

Her companion merely smiled revealing those few, brave teeth.

She stopped in mid-sentence. He was beginning to shimmer and it began to occur to her that he was probably going to take a less usual route out of this prison.

She pushed away all that she'd been taught in science. School and 'normal' life were becoming less relevant by the hour.

Above them the boy waited impatiently, 'Well, do you want to come up or not?'

Hairy Face spoke quietly, 'I'm goin', but not with you lass. The hound and I 'ave a different destination.'

He gestured to Gawain, 'Get your friend up there, we'll be fine. You'd better be quick lass, time is runnin' out!'

Tamar took a long, hard look at Hairy Face and the dog. There was a lot she wanted to say to this strange little man, but Hairy Face looked at her and shook his head. He didn't need the words.

'Go on lass, quick now!'

For once Tamar did as she was told and, turning to Gawain, slipped her arm around him.

'Come on,' she said and leant over to pull him up. She set her teeth as another spike of barbed pain reminded her of her own injury, and prayed that the watch, hidden in her pocket, wouldn't start chiming. 'We're going on the deck for some fresh air, it'll do you good.'

Gawain could hear the words but his legs didn't want to obey him.

Tamar whispered, 'Come on Gawain, you've *got* to do it. It's our only chance.'

He groaned but the urgency in her voice filtered through.

His head hammered but, with Tamar's help, he hauled himself upright and shuffled towards the ladder.

...

Porth Talant

In Porth Talant bay, Nick opened the front door of Dywana's cottage and heard Arthur's aunt call, '*Comero weeth.*'

'Yeah, thanks Dywana,' he said quietly.

A few cats still lingered, he was grateful for that, and Dywana's cat was sitting on the beach wall. It might only be a cat but he always felt safer when it was around.

As far as he could see the beach was unoccupied, the only movement was the waves lapping lazily against the sand and the pebbles. He looked behind him at the white cottage, sitting in its rose-filled garden, and at the hills beyond the house. Trees clung to the slopes, ancient woods disguising the folds in the land and obscuring the secret paths used by animals. Nick wondered if there was anyone, or anything, there. He glanced up at the sky but it was empty, there was no sign of the crow which probably meant that the Crow Man wouldn't be around either.

Nick turned away towards the lane and made his way from the beach-front path to the narrow road, and from bright sunlight into deep shade. High, dense hedges rose up on either side of the lane, topped by leafy trees reaching out to one another above him.

He walked a little way and stopped. His neck prickled as if someone was watching him. He walked a few more paces and stopped to check the road behind him, but it was empty.

Muttering to himself to get a grip, he strode on determined to ignore the feeling but then he heard them, faint footsteps keeping in step with his own.

He spun around, he was right, there *was* someone there because he saw a grey shadow melt into the hedge beside a gnarled oak tree.

Nick swallowed hard, delved into his pocket and drew out the dragon which just sat looking at him sleepily, blinking in the daylight.

'Now, Little fella,' he whispered, 'let's see if you're as good at defence as you think you are.'

The dragon didn't stir, but a rustle in the hedge woke him up and instantly he was on full alert and sitting up. There was the faintest crunch of leaves as Nick's stalker moved - and the dragon took off.

He flew straight as a dart towards the noise. A tiny, fiery missile. Seconds later there was an explosion of white sparks and orange flames marking the position of the invisible spy. Then there was a shout of pain coupled with a '*woomph*', followed by silence and a swirl of grey smoke curling up from the spot where Nick's stalker had been hidden.

Triumphantly, the little dragon emerged from the bushes, a little scorched around his jaw but with pride leaking from every scale. He swooped towards Nick, flew around him once and landed neatly on his shoulder. Nick waited for the invisible spy to emerge, but there wasn't even the tiniest of movements or the slightest of sounds from the spot where the smoke still lingered.

A thought took hold - surely the dragon hadn't managed to kill his follower!

Nick edged towards the oak tree, cloaked in opaque shadows, and the unmistakable scent of burnt flesh wafted towards him. There, in a hollow in the hedge beside the tree, was a shoe, at least Nick thought it was a shoe, but there was nothing else.

No-one. No thing. Nothing.

He peered behind the trunk of the ancient tree but the hedge was solid and impenetrable, knitted together with prickly hawthorn and holly, no one could get through that. Nick bent down and retrieved the shoe and inspected it carefully, wondering what clues it could give him.

The shoe was made from soft, red leather and was more of a short ankle boot than an ordinary shoe; furthermore it had an extremely long, pointed toe that curled up at the end. He turned it over in his hands and examined the stitching which, although it was beautiful, was slightly irregular as if it had been made by hand. And then he remembered a picture he'd seen of a court jester and realised that the man in the drawing had been wearing shoes like this.

So someone had been here, wearing this boot, and they'd disappeared into thin air. He swallowed. This was way beyond anything else he'd experienced. Nick put his hand up to the dragon, now sitting on his shoulder, and stroked its back while he thought. The creature nuzzled his hand with its still-warm snout and made a deep, contented clicking in its throat, the closest a dragon could get to a purr.

'Well done, boy,' Nick said. 'I'm glad I found you but I bet that someone, somewhere, isn't so happy about it.'

He looked around again, but he was sure that now he and the dragon were alone.

'Come on boy, we'd better get there before anyone else does. You might have some more work to do before too long.'

He lifted the dragon from his shoulder and opened his pocket. The dragon climbed in and within seconds faint, dragon snores rose out of his jacket. Even though the dragon had only come to life in the last day or so, he was already very much at home. Nick looked up the steep lane scored into the hillside and, taking a deep breath, set off again determined to leave the problem of the disappearing person (if it was a person), behind him.

Chapter 17

~ Mysteries revealed ~

Arthur heard Dywana's words to Nick as he left and he saw the deep colours that accompanied them, they were purples and browns which meant that she was worried. He heard her talking to someone in the kitchen but it sounded a very one-sided conversation because he couldn't hear another voice. He turned back to the scroll, he needed to find out what the rest of the verse said before he went.

He was certain that he knew the lake that was pictured on the scroll, it was all beginning to make sense now. That, and the meeting with Bedivere on the moor, it was coming together like the final pieces of a jigsaw.

The water on the silent lake rippled, a breeze disturbed the surface, then a hand appeared in the centre of the lake – and the hand was holding a sword. Finally the rest of the verse flooded across the parchment.

'From water she comes,
a sword in her hand.
The bearer's The One
who shall rescue the land.'

The Lady of the Lake. Of course, he should have known! Bedivere had given the sword back to her for safe-keeping. But now Arthur needed it. The sword was vital if he was going to be able to fulfil his part in this quest and time was running out. He stood up to leave but as he did the book turned a page to a new picture.

A man's face looked out at him from the book, he was wearing a black mask with holes roughly cut out for his eyes. Arthur stared and, as he watched, the eyes blinked and a slow, menacing smile spread across the face. The masked stranger fixed Arthur with a look that chilled him to the bone and the golden sword, hanging around Arthur's neck, froze. It was so cold that he could feel it welding itself to his chest. He gasped – and the man's smile grew. Then with a *'thwack'*, the book slammed shut.

The ship on the windowsill rocked wildly and Lightning, sitting at Arthur's feet, had his brown eyes fixed on his master. He was waiting for his next move, but Arthur was frozen by the menace that had reached out to him from the page. He could actually feel his heart thumping as the adrenaline coursed through his veins.

The sword had seared its mark on his flesh but with the book closed, it was warming again. Shaking, he peeled it away from his chest and peered down to see that where the sword had been lying was an angry, red scar. However as he inspected the wound, deep words penetrated his thoughts, but this time it wasn't just one voice but a chorus of voices.

He could make out John Oliver and he thought that he could hear Jago. Dywana was definitely there but most powerful of all was Michael. They were trying to comfort him because somehow they knew what had taken place. They were also preparing him for what lay ahead. The last words he heard were those he'd heard often in the past few days, *'Comero weeth'* – 'Take care', and then both the colours and the voices faded.

Taking a deep breath, Arthur looked down at Lightning, 'Are you ready for this boy?'

The dog wagged his tail enthusiastically.

'I'm not sure that I am.'

He reached for his bag, glanced around the room, and delved into the box holding all his treasures.

There at the bottom was the whistle, given to him last year by Michael. Arthur checked the golden thread and hung it around his neck. Then he picked up the model knight given to him by Great-Uncle Lance. He couldn't imagine that it would be of any use but it would just be comforting to have it and to be reminded of the people who cared about this cause. Part of him wished that he'd taken up Nick's offer of the dragon, but it was too late for that now. It was him and Lightning against the rest – whoever they might be.

'Come on then boy,' Arthur said, opening the door, and Lightning rushed past him and down the stairs. He was keen, even if his owner wasn't.

Dywana was waiting for him by the front door and from the kitchen a familiar, but long-dead, voice called out, 'Take care boy, and keep that model safe too!'

A smile flitted across Dywana's face at Arthur's expression.

'T''is your great-uncle, he lives on in the paintin' – for now.'

Arthur looked from Dywana to the kitchen door.

'No,' he said slowly. 'That can't be him!'

Dywana raised her eyebrows, 'Can't it?'

And again Arthur's world shifted.

A voice from the kitchen boomed, 'Go on lad, we'll meet at the appointed time. You've got work to do, we can't waste time chattin'.'

The voice added, 'Proud of you lad though, I'm proud of you.'

His aunt was holding the front door open, 'Go on Arthur.'

Then she rested her hand on his shoulder and, before he could change his mind, she'd gently pushed him outside and closed the door behind him, leaving him standing alone in the fading light.

Arthur looked around as Nick had earlier. All he could see was a lady sitting on the rocks at the far side of the beach but she didn't appear to be aware of him. Somehow she reminded him of that strange history teacher who'd appeared at their school last year, however it was difficult to make her out in the gloom. She appeared to be writing, which struck him as odd, but he turned away with his thoughts full of his great-uncle and that masked face.

Purple clouds rolled across the sky and lightning flashed on the horizon, while further out to sea, thunder rumbled. A storm was brewing.

Arthur knew the signs. The dark powers were flexing their muscles ready for battle and to fight for the ultimate prize. He heaved a sigh as he remembered the fight for the life of little Kensa last year, he hoped that no innocent child would be drawn into this conflict.

He looked up at the hills behind the cottage and at the cliffs either side of the bay.

At first Arthur couldn't see anything unusual but then, through the trees, he caught a glimpse of a flash of black. It wasn't so much a colour as more of an absence of it, as if all the light had been sucked into a black hole. He shuddered, he had a long way to go and already he could feel them gathering. Well, he'd just have to face them, he hadn't any choice, and the minutes were ticking away. So taking a deep breath, Arthur slung his bag onto his shoulder, whistled quietly to Lightning and set off towards whoever – or whatever might be waiting.

Meanwhile out at sea a small boat was approaching a sailing ship, accompanied by dolphins arcing out of the water and a seal bobbing around and under the oars.

...

'Come on,' Tamar encouraged Gawain. 'You can do it.'

Under her breath she said, 'We've got to get out of here!'

She pushed him up the ladder while the spotty boy waited. She was certain that she could feel the pocket watch winding itself up, ready to chime.

'Not now,' she thought desperately. 'Just wait a few minutes.'

'Well. Are you going to help, or are you just going to stand there watching?' Tamar asked the boy.

'It's you who wanted to come up 'ere,' the boy said, belligerently. 'T'wasn't my idea. Besides they said I 'ave to watch you.'

To emphasise the point he twirled the pistol, or rather tried to twirl it, but his finger got in the way.

'Ow, now I've got me finger stuck!' he cried, dancing around the deck. 'Darn thing, I knew they'd given me an old one.'

He swore, shaking his hand, and gingerly slid the pistol off his trapped finger. He glanced nervously towards the living quarters but no one appeared.

Tamar said drily, 'Yeah, I can see this ship's safe with you to protect it.'

However her irony was lost on him. 'Yeah, 'cause I'm their first line of defence,' their jailer said proudly, examining his finger.

From the cabin below her, Tamar heard Hairy Face snort and exclaim, 'T'is good to know there are boys like 'im in Kernow. Fine men are hard to find.'

Despite her circumstances Tamar giggled, and cast a look over her shoulder at her fellow prisoner, but her laughter died on her lips because Hairy Face was only just visible, and the dog had already gone. As she watched him, Hairy face managed a blurry wink and a gummy grin before he too finally disappeared. There was a soft sigh, like a breeze through a tree, and a heavy clank as his chains fell to the floor. He was free. Her companion had left his prison in his own, very individual, way. All that remained was the dog's cracked bowl and its master's iron shackles.

Tamar swallowed, because it's not every day that someone dissolves in front of you.

Then Gawain was sick. Very sick. It splashed across the deck and onto the boy's bare feet - a river of vomit.

The boy leapt back, 'Oi!' he yelled.

'Sorry,' whispered Gawain. 'Couldn't help it.'

'That's disgustin',' the boy carried on. 'It's all over my feet!'

'Sorry,' Gawain muttered again.

Tamar looked at Gawain, he looked terrible and his head had started to leak blood again.

'Look,' she said to the boy, 'if you get some water, I'll clear it up.'

She turned to Gawain and instructed, 'Get close to the rail, then if you're sick again you can be sick over the side.'

But under her breath she whispered, 'That was brilliant, I couldn't have done it better if I'd tried.'

She looked behind her. The boy was examining the deck and his feet glistening with Gawain's vomit. He'd turned a pale shade of green. It looked like it could be catching.

'Go on!' she commanded the boy. 'I don't mind sick, and you'll be in trouble if you leave it.'

Spotty Face didn't need any more encouragement and, mumbling something about that's what happens when you try and be nice to people, took himself off in pursuit of a bucket.

Gawain leant over the rail. 'Really sorry,' he said again.

'It's okay, forget it,' Tamar said. 'The main thing is, how are we going to get off here before they find out that we're on the deck?'

She knew that at any minute one of their captors could appear – then this one, precious chance would be lost.

'A boat,' Gawain muttered groggily.

'Yeah, we're on a boat,' Tamar answered patiently.

'No, look,' he said, pointing, and was sick again.

She heard the faint putter of an outboard engine and looked down. A boat had crept into sight, furthermore she recognised its occupant - it was Jago. At that moment she heard raised voices from one of the cabins. The spotty boy had obviously been found to be away from his station.

'Oh no,' she groaned.

She looked around desperately.

There was another round of shouting - they'd be up here any minute. Then an idea struck her and running back to the hatch, she seized the ladder and dragged it to the rail.

'Quick,' she said to her friend, as she hoisted it over the rails and hooked it to the side.

Gawain took in the ladder and for the briefest of moments the mist that was clouding his thoughts cleared.

'Might be sick again,' he said with a weak grin.

'Don't care,' Tamar said. 'Just go!'

Grunting with the effort he clambered up and over the rails. Jago was ready below him, steadying the little boat against the side of the ship.

Tamar glanced behind her to see that both the Crow Man and the woman were already emerging from the cabin, and that a dark shape was flitting towards her.

'Quick!' she hissed. 'They're coming.'

Gawain fell into the bottom of the boat and Jago shouted, 'Come on lass - jump!'

Tamar looked behind her again and her heart missed a beat, the woman was striding towards her with the Crow Man at her side. She'd always hated heights but it looked like the luxury of choice had been removed and, with a deep breath, Tamar scrambled onto the ship's rails.

Chapter 18

~ The Highwayman ~

Nick pushed the gate open. He listened intently but all he could hear was the wind and the waves far below, and the gentle snoring of a tiny, green dragon.

He put his hand into the other pocket and felt the soft leather of the shoe left behind by his stalker and a thought struck him. The sword and chain hadn't changed temperature when he was being followed so whoever had been following him couldn't have been a threat, but how could anyone disappear like that?

He looked up the gravelled path leading past the church and into the graveyard, it was late evening and even though it was summer the light was already fading. Each footstep took him further in, further into the territory of the dead, and dark shadows reached out towards him from every gravestone. His steps sounded too loud, amplified by the still night, as if every crunch on the gravel was an announcement of his arrival.

'Come on,' he said to himself, 'you know you don't believe in ghosts.' But it was then that he saw the leaves in the hedge which bordered the graveyard, trembling.

Nick froze, his heart racing, and peered into the gloom. He tried to conjure up logical thoughts about mice or other wildlife, when there was a rustle accompanied by the tiniest of movements. It could have been something completely natural, but he had a feeling that whatever was disturbing the vegetation was unlikely to be a normal mammal.

'Right boy,' Nick said softly, 'time to practise your flame-throwing again.'

He lifted the little dragon out of his pocket but this time the creature didn't sit up, he just stayed curled up on his hand.

'Go on!' Nick said urgently. 'You can't sleep now.'

Still the animal didn't move, he actually looked a little grumpy at being woken up a second time. Then the leaves in the hedge quivered and parted and a green eye held Nick's gaze.

'What are you doing? You're meant to be a fighter!' Nick hissed to the sleeping dragon.

A huge, black paw appeared followed by a powerful leg, then the rest of the animal broke out from the hedge. Nick had heard stories of the Beast that was supposed to roam the moors, he'd even seen blurred photos, but none of them had conveyed its size and power. Silently it prowled towards him until it was so close that Nick could hear its breathing.

By now Nick was incapable of any movement. He remembered all too well that fateful night on the moors a year ago when Matearnas had fallen to her death. He'd caught a glimpse of something then, and it had looked remarkably like the creature approaching him now.

But at that moment it started to purr - and the purr grew. The ground rumbled beneath Nick's feet as the creature moved towards him. It was so huge that its great, green eyes were on a level with his, however his fear was dissolving because the cat was making it very clear that it was on his side.

The creature gazed deep into Nick's eyes and held his gaze. Then it pushed its head against Nick's shoulder, its whiskers brushing his face and its breath warm against his skin, before turning away towards the gate and quietly padding away.

Nick watched it disappear, his thoughts a jumble of questions woven through with a glow of warm reassurance. Interestingly, Dragon hadn't been either afraid or poised ready to attack the beast. Perhaps, Nick thought, he should learn to watch Dragon's reactions.

However Nick's reflections were short-lived because they were interrupted by a faint noise which sounded something like a far-off drum beat.

He listened to the reverberations filling the valley below him, they were growing louder with every second, and he was puzzled until he understood that they weren't coming from just one place.

Nick looked at the gate and muttered, 'Now what?' as he realised that the beats were moving, and that they were coming his way, pounding up the hill towards him.

The sound swelled and grew, echoing off the hills, until it was right outside the churchyard gate and then it stopped. There was a whinny as a horse was bought to a halt in the lane and then - silence. However this was not the peaceful silence of a few minutes before, this was a dead silence.

Nick waited with his heart thudding and his chest tightening, and speculated on what would appear. He had a brief flashback to the meeting with that woman who'd been watching Tamar in Porth Pyra. His body and mind still bore the memory of the ice world she'd plunged him into and the sheer misery he'd felt. Only this time he was alone in a graveyard, with not another soul around. Well, at least not a living one.

A stench blew in on the breeze. It was the smell of death. Something was walking up the path, crunching on the gravel between the gravestones, and this time the dragon was on full alert.

A figure came into view and Nick felt his breath being sucked out of his body. If the beast had been for him, Nick was in no doubt that this apparition was against him and, just as the woman who had been following Tamar was dressed from head to toe in black, so was this creature. But this black was far, far deeper. It radiated evil.

'You wait alone.'

The voice was bone-dry.

Nick didn't respond. How could you talk to a skeleton dressed as a highwayman?

'You may wait and protect this place but they will never come,' the skeleton said. His bony finger pushed his tricorn hat back into place. Presumably it had been dislodged while riding.

Nick still said nothing.

The creature rearranged its cloak and checked his riding boots. This was probably the most fashion conscious skeleton Nick was ever likely to meet. In fact it was probably the *only* skeleton Nick would ever meet.

'Riding hard is the death of good clothes!' the skeleton said - and attempted a grin, but it's difficult to see if a skeleton is grinning. You need muscles and flesh for a successful smile.

Nick cleared his throat but he couldn't think of any contribution he could make because his brain, as well as his limbs, was paralysed. How could anyone cope with a speaking skeleton?

But in an instant the skeleton's attitude had changed and his brief attempt at humour was abandoned. He fiddled with a pistol hanging to one side and with a riding crop swinging in his other bony hand.

The skeleton fixed Nick with an eye-less stare, 'You may think that you are protected, that you are special, but you are merely one of the four Guardians – and you are alone. There is no one else here for you.'

Swishing the crop thoughtfully, he said, 'You shouldn't be afraid though, I was always an excellent shot. So the end won't be painful.'

Looking at the graves surrounding them, he added, 'And such a convenient place to die!'

Nick could feel the dragon tensing, ready to launch, but even so a sense of hopelessness washed over him. He was such a tiny dragon and anyway he couldn't see how fire could be of any use against bone. But as these thoughts threatened to overwhelm him there was a noise, a scraping, and the skeleton's words died away. If there had been blood in its body it would have frozen, and Nick was certain that its skull blanched. The skeleton's empty eye sockets focused on something just behind him and Nick felt the dragon begin to relax.

The bony highwayman's hands stilled and he spoke to whatever was at Nick's back, 'So, you have been awoken.'

A sound like stones being scraped together greeted these words. The skeleton was silent. He appeared to be considering his next move. Nick had the feeling that whatever it had been planning had just been compromised.

Although the dragon had relaxed when it had become clear that they weren't alone against the bone ranger, it still sat on Nick's hand – ready to attack. Suddenly he felt its body tense and then it had taken off. He watched it soar towards the heavens, a green-winged arrow cutting through the air.

It climbed higher and higher until it was a tiny green dot against the deepening blue of the evening sky, and then it started to circle.

Nick tracked it sweeping around high above them before starting to spiral down towards the skeletal highwayman, and then there was a flash of fire as the skeleton's hat burst into flame.

A roar of rage broke the silence. 'My hat! That flying rat has destroyed my hat!'

The skeleton, his hat still on fire, gripped his riding crop and lashed out at the dragon, but it was too fast for him. The more he struck out, the faster the dragon darted, and it was then that Nick felt and heard the laughter. It sounded like boulders being flung together, or a river flowing over rocks.

There were no words, just sounds, but Nick didn't turn around to find out what was making the noise, he didn't dare. It was quite bad enough to be watching an angry skeleton wearing a burning hat, trying to catch a flying dragon.

But then the furious skeleton appeared to become aware of the laughter, because he suddenly ceased trying to catch his winged enemy and, bones clanking, swivelled towards the sound.

Fixing the object behind Nick with a stony, blank-eyed stare, he said, 'You will regret your laughter. You are still without the sword – and without it neither you nor this land are protected. The sea will not be rid of its memories and this land will never know peace.'

Calmly he took off his hat, extinguished the last of the flames, and carefully replaced it on the top of his skull. Wisps of smoke rose from the brim.

The dragon had landed on Nick's shoulder and was now busy washing itself, content with a job well done. It appeared to be getting the hang of fire-throwing.

Addressing Nick, the would-be highwayman said quietly, 'Your wait will be a long and lonely one.'

There was a crash of thunder and the skeleton looked towards the sky.

'Ah, and so it starts; the final act of the play. I am called to another place. Your Guide, your friend and leader, is on his way and I wish to accompany him.'

Sheet lightning flashed across the darkening horizon.

The skeleton rearranged his cloak and tucked the pistol into his belt, 'I can promise you that your waiting will come to nothing.'

Then with a flourish, and with as much dignity as he could muster under his still-smouldering hat, he turned and stalked out of the churchyard.

Nick watched him go and waited, wondering if he'd return, but hooves galloping up the lane away from the churchyard reassured him. He realised that although the evening was cool, he was sweating. The highwayman's threats echoed in his head and for the first time Nick questioned whether Arthur would make it. He had to. All of Cornwall's future – and its past - depended on him.

He turned towards the sea and saw a carved, stone angel standing on a plinth. In the half-light it looked as if it could be alive and for a moment Nick wondered if that was where the laughter had been coming from. He brushed that thought aside, he wasn't even going to go there, and walked to the edge of the churchyard bordering the cliff. The dragon sat on his shoulder and together they looked out over the sea. Storm clouds massed across the bay and a tall-masted ship rolled and swayed in the strengthening gale. A little boat detached itself from the ship's side and it was then that Nick heard the scream.

...

Looking behind her as she teetered on the hand-rail of the ship, Tamar saw the woman and the Crow Man striding across the deck towards her. She looked down at the boat far below.

A shout from Jago shattered her thoughts, 'Jump lass!'

She hesitated, it was a long drop and she didn't like heights, but another quick glance across the deck decided her. Tamar had never been the object of pure hate but murder was written all over her captor's face. One way or another, the future didn't look bright.

Tamar swallowed as an icy finger touched her wrist, and she jumped.

A scream pierced the air as she fell – and kept on falling.

Jago watched Tamar dropping through space. He tried as best he could to break her fall but she was unconscious before she hit the boards. There was a sickening thud and a crack of bones - then silence.

The little boat rocked violently, threatening to capsize, but Jago didn't wait. Instead, clamping down on his immediate impulse to go to the aid of the girl, he gunned the boat's outboard motor and turned towards the shore. Every second was vital if he was going to save these Guardians. Angry shouts echoed behind him, and then he heard the deep words, fury-filled and packed with hatred. They were telling him that if he was caught he'd be dead.

But he already knew that.

Crashes of thunder echoed around the bay and flashes of lightning lit up the darkening sky. The sea began to heave and waves broke over the side of the boat, soaking its occupants, but neither Tamar nor Gawain moved.

Blocking the violent words slicing through his brain, Jago concentrated on getting the little boat back to shore. He glanced at Gawain, his colour was deathly pale again, and checked Tamar. Her arm was twisted under her back and her breathing was alarmingly shallow. It was not only the fall that had hurt her, but the woman's deadly touch.

Jago glanced over the side of the boat and then he saw them, the long-dead. Hands reached up to him from the dark ocean, the fingers white, dead flesh. Pleading eyes beseeched him to rescue them. Eyes filled with longing, begging to be released from their watery grave.

'Be gone!' Jago shouted. 'You are no more than memories.'

Still, hands reached up towards the boat. A lightning bolt forked from the sky to the sea and the water sizzled around them. Jago had never seen the sea boil before.

With his guard lowered, deep words from the Lady of Clehy penetrated his brain, 'We can stir up the memories, we can add to those in the sea. Who do you think you are to defy my wishes? You alone have no strength, only a misplaced loyalty. This land – and its people - belong to me.'

Jago sent deep words back but he knew that his power was no match for the woman, and she knew it too.

Another lightning bolt shot out of the heavens but this time it was followed by a splash at the side of the boat. There was a shower of rainbow drops and bodies arcing out of the sea. But these were not the bodies of long-dead people but of dolphins, leaping over the boat and diving beneath it. They filled the air with their clicks as they sang to each other. Tamar stirred, Gawain groaned and, for the first time that day, Jago smiled. They were not alone.

It was then that the chiming started - in perfect time with the dolphins' clicks. It sounded as though it was coming from far away, which it probably was. After all, it had travelled over many centuries to make it this far. The chiming was a triumphant march, a celebration, and the dolphins leapt even higher.

Jago chuckled, 'So Zephaniah has accomplished 'is mission – and old Hairy Harry has played 'is part. The Time-Keeper is the girl. Who would 'ave thought it? Times are changing!'

The watch continued to chime its melodic defiance in Tamar's pocket, before breaking into another tune, a sea shanty.

'Now someone's got a sense of 'umour,' Jago said softly to himself, steering the boat past the rocks.

Chapter 19

~ Flight of the Memories ~

Arthur trudged up the steep lane with its towering hedges bordering both sides of the road, and wondered again if he'd make it in time. He had to – everything depended on it.

He thought about Nick, alone in the graveyard, and of Tamar and Gawain's disappearance. Were they alright? His mind veered away from all the possible outcomes, and from his first-hand knowledge of the Crow Man's cruelty, instead he clung to the certainty that others would be fighting their corner. He was so deep in thought that at first he didn't hear the hooves galloping up the lane behind him, it was only Lightening's whine that alerted him.

Arthur looked around, but the horse and its rider weren't yet in view. Then he surveyed the darkening sky and knew that no normal person would ever take the risk of riding their horse in this light, and an inner voice urged him to hide. He glanced at the stone walls topped with wild hedges on either side of the lane, but they were too high to climb over and there were no gaps in the hedge large enough to conceal both him and Lightning.

In desperation he backed into the stony hedge in the vain hope that the few twigs and bushes growing there might provide them with some sort of cover - and felt a hand pull him into an earthy hollow which, a moment before, he could have sworn hadn't existed. He looked behind him but no-one was there.

And then he was certain that he heard a muttered, 'Sorry!'

Was it a trick of the light, or had he really caught a glimpse of a woolly hat?

There was the tiniest '*crack*' followed by a '*woomph*', and the hat and its wearer disappeared.

Arthur shook his head trying to come to terms with a vanishing ally - it wasn't the easiest of ideas to absorb. Then he tucked Lightning behind his legs and whispered, 'Quiet boy.'

His dog looked up at him, his brown eyes reproachful. He knew he needed to be quiet, he didn't need Arthur to tell him.

'Sorry,' Arthur apologised automatically.

He peered through the leaves concealing them to see that the horse and its rider had rounded the bend in the lane and were cantering up the hill. And that the rider was a skeleton.

Arthur drew further back into the hollow, his heart's pounding joining with the hoof beats' drumming, and his eyes wide at the shock of this fresh horror. On his chest the sword froze, fusing itself to his skin once again and he understood that he'd seen this face before. It was the face that the book had shown him in the safety of his bedroom. Only this time it wasn't trapped between the covers of a book but galloping up the hill towards him. Fleetingly, Arthur recalled his first meeting with Matearnas, and how he'd then thought that he could never possibly encounter anyone, or anything, so evil. Yet this creature was far, far worse. If Matearnas and the Crow Man had exuded evil, this apparition was evil personified– and it was dressed as a highwayman!

Then Arthur heard it speaking and realised that the skeleton was grumbling.

'Darn dragon, setting my hat on fire,' he was saying.

Arthur caught sight of wisps of smoke coiling away from the brim of the skeleton's hat and, despite his racing heart-beat, grinned. So Nick and the dragon had already met this creature and it sounded as though they'd come out on top. The skeleton stopped muttering. He halted his mount, tilted his skull back and sniffed at the night air. He looked around him, his empty eye-sockets boring into the darkness.

Slowly, the long-dead highwayman reached for his pistol and commanded, 'Be still!'

The horse shifted nervously.

'Quiet!' its master ordered, scanning the hedge.

There was a rustling and an unsuspecting shrew scuttled out from under a bush and immediately became an ex-shrew. The highwayman might be a skeleton but he was a deadly shot.

'My senses are dulled,' the skeleton said. 'I've wasted my time on vermin.'

He regarded the ever-darkening sky through the overhanging trees and remarked to himself, 'The time approaches, we must make haste.'

Pushing the pistol back into his belt, the skeleton pressed his hat low over his skull and squeezed his bone knees into the horse's side. The animal, eyes staring, whinnied and shot off as if he had the devil at his back. Arthur listened as the hoof beats died away and waited for his heart to resume its natural rhythm. Their hide-away had worked. Whoever had helped him into it had probably saved his life.

Then glancing down to the quivering dog at his side, Arthur said, 'It's alright boy. He's gone... for the time anyway.'

He stroked Lightning's head and mused, 'But I think I know where he's heading and I don't think that he's going to be alone up there. It looks like there's going to be quite a reception committee.'

Shifting the bag onto his other shoulder, Arthur glanced up at the first star in the evening sky. Time was against him and the importance of his mission had just been horribly emphasised. With a shake of his head he weighed up the alternative routes; there really was only one option.

'Right boy, we'd better take the short cut, time's running out. We'll have to forget the train and Nick's bike. It's going to have to be the Smugglers' Way.'

This old path was grim at the best of times – and this wasn't the best of times - but he hadn't any choice. He stepped out of their earthy hide-away and examined

223

it. Whoever, or whatever, had pulled him in there had taken the most unusual way out.

'Come on then boy,' Arthur said, 'we can't stay here, we've got an appointment.'

He turned, trying to banish the problem of the disappearance of their invisible helper, and a highwayman that was also a skeleton, and began to climb the hill. He'd tackle those problems later because, right now, he had to get to the most important meeting of his life.

It was a punishing, almost vertical, slope. The adrenalin that had flooded his veins was wearing off and his legs were doing a passable imitation of jelly. Every step was an effort. He laboured up the lane, desperately trying to dismiss the negative voices which warned of the consequences if he should fail.

He could just make out the muted song of the waves on Porth Talant beach far below and behind him. He wondered whether anything was happening at Dywana's cottage or if she too had other business. Nothing would surprise him because she was proving to be the most unlikely aunt. Not at all the aunt he'd known as he'd grown up.

A soft whisper, and a branch above him shivered as a pair of white wings took flight. He looked up and caught a pair of large, dark eyes looking directly into his. Arthur tracked the owl's silent flight beneath the leaf-lined branches and watched as it glided towards an opening half-way up the hill and settled on a post. The bird was marking the entrance to the Smugglers' Way.

Usually the path was well hidden because it was rarely used by walkers and only local people were aware of its existence. In the past it had been used by smugglers to transport their illegal goods from the coast to villages inland, well away from the watchful eyes of the law. The path remaining secret would have meant the difference between life and death because the penalty for smuggling had been hanging. With these thoughts swirling through his mind, and images of bodies swinging from a creaking gibbet, Arthur found himself at the path's entrance. As soon as he arrived, the bird hooted once and took off, sweeping silently through the velvet night and leaving Arthur alone. He looked around. He couldn't see anyone but he was certain that he was being watched. He waited for a few seconds, allowing his breathing to settle down, and listened for anything that would indicate that someone else was there. But, apart from birds calling to each other, there was silence.

Eventually, satisfied as he could be that they really were alone, he turned into the gap in the hedge. He'd arrived at the hidden entrance to the Smugglers' Way.

'Okay boy, are you ready?'

Arthur looked up the dark path.

'Doesn't exactly look inviting does it?'

The dog barked.

'I know, I know, we've got to go. Come on then.'

With a final look behind him, he took a deep breath and set off.

He walked quickly, occasionally breaking into a trot whenever the path was smooth enough. The further they journeyed, the darker it became with the branches of oak, hazel and beech trees meeting high above them. Gradually the well-worn path dropped down, sinking even lower under its leafy roof, until they were walking on rock. The earth must have been worn away through the centuries until only the bedrock was left, polished by hundreds of pairs of feet hurrying along its length.

Arthur knew that this path had been used by smugglers and usually he would have found this exciting, but now he hated to even start to imagine what memories might lie in wait.

Pushing these thoughts away he pressed on, determined not to lose another minute, when a squawk and a crunch in the branches of a tree ahead of them stopped him dead in his tracks. A blackbird flew out of the tree-cover calling once. There was an answering call further along the path and Arthur had the uncanny feeling that their progress was being monitored. He thought about the seal appearing in the bay and the dolphins swimming beside John Oliver's boat and, of course, the cats. An awful lot of animals appeared to be involved.

He checked the sky, what he could see of it through the trees, and then he peered at his watch and his stomach turned. He knew that he had to be there by midnight but at this rate he'd never make it. The voices during the storm in Porth Talant bay came rushing back to him and another piece of the puzzle fell into place. He wasn't only being asked to protect Cornwall as it was now, but to help the memories of its past.

As he thought of those memories, something pressed past him and his flesh crawled. There was a flash of a foot and a glimpse of a finger and it was gone to be traded for another half-formed shape, a cloaked figure which turned its face towards him before disappearing. Then the path was alive with ancient memories rushing towards Arthur; a hand, a face, a leg, none of them complete, just hints of the people they'd once been. But not one of them paid even a passing interest in the boy with his dog. Lightning whined, his ears flat against his head and his tail low as the apparitions silently dashed along the ancient way. However, Arthur's initial gut-wrenching fear faded as he noticed that all of the half-people were running in the opposite direction, away from the moor, and that he was no more than an obstacle to them.

He stood, watching the fragments of previous inhabitants rush past when one shape came to a halt. It stood in front of him and gradually assembled itself, starting at the feet and working upwards until it was complete. Then it bowed.

'Zephaniah Jenner at your service, Sire,' it said.

Arthur stared.

'You are younger than I expected,' the memory said thoughtfully, fiddling with his moustache. 'But I have been told that you are The One.'

Arthur was vaguely aware of the sword around his neck gradually warming as if it had recognised an old friend and, whereas Lightning had been standing petrified during the flight of the memories, now he was wagging his tail.

Arthur relaxed.

The figures around them were thinning out; although most of them had been fairly thin in the first place.

Zephaniah rubbed the end of his curled moustache between his fore-finger and thumb.

'Sire,' he said, and appeared to be savouring the word, 'the Writer has given me the immense honour of accompanying you.'

Arthur had no idea who this strange apparition, dressed in a frock coat with such an impressive moustache, was talking about. However a lot of things didn't make sense. All he knew was that he had to make it to the lake by midnight and that was all that mattered.

Nothing else, however weird, could be allowed to hinder his quest. He'd schedule his nervous breakdown for later.

Zephaniah nodded, hearing his thoughts. 'We'll do it Sire. Other help has been sent.'

Then Arthur heard the deep words, but these had a distinctly horsey twang and were interspersed with whinnies. A white shape glimmered through the darkness. It was a horse.

Zephaniah chuckled, 'Ah, Argo, a timely arrival.' Turning to Arthur he said, 'You see Sire? You will not have to walk. Argo will carry you to the meeting. No horse in all of Kernow is as fleet of foot.'

The horse was positioning himself next to a rock, ready for Arthur to climb onto his back as Zephaniah said, 'A pleasure and an honour to meet again, Argo.'

And the horse was returning his greetings, but by now Arthur couldn't tell which part of the conversation was being conducted in the deep words and which part was spoken in his normal tongue. However, to be honest it didn't matter; a horse speaking either way was a first for him.

. . .

The Watchers stood side by side on the cliff above Porth Talant bay.

They'd Watched the little boat push away from the ship and heard the outboard motor gun into life as the storm clouds grew and rolled towards the land. They'd witnessed Nick's departure from the cottage, and Servo had returned from his close encounter with Arthur and the skeletal highwayman.

Viatoris looked out to sea, 'The boy, the Chosen One, is safe?'

The other Watcher nodded, thinking guiltily of the help he'd given Arthur. He knew he'd broken the Rule because he'd become involved. Then he caught sight of his companion's feet. One of the pointed shoes was missing, and he looked at Viatoris' face, one of his eyebrows was singed and he was sure that he could smell burnt hair.

'And you have met the dragon?'

Viatoris shifted uncomfortably and nodded, but his companion said, 'It seems that you are not the only one to be the object of the dragon's fury. The highwayman, too, has been hurt. Or at least his pride has been scorched.'

'So, at present all four are safe.'

'At present – yes.'

The boat plunged through the sea, lightning forking down either side it. The Watchers were quiet as they listened to the silent screams and Watched the beseeching hands reaching from deep beneath the waves.

'He has to succeed if the memories are to be stilled and healed,' Viatoris mused.

Servo nodded, and then he swore softly as he felt a tug, 'I'm being summoned back to Egypt. I have to go, I have no choice.'

Viatoris said, 'In that case, I will Watch by the lake.'

The walker nodded, the air crackled – and he was gone.

Chapter 20

~ Lancelot ~

Jago sent deep words towards the cottage. The door opened and a figure, wrapping a shawl tightly around her shoulders, hurried through the storm.

Jago leapt over the side of the boat into the shallow waters, and began to drag it onto the sand. Dywana arriving at the water's edge, surveyed Jago's passengers. Encrusted blood clung to Gawain's hair and face and his wound still oozed, but his colour was returning. Tamar, on the other hand, was chalk-white. She was leaning back against the side of the boat with her eyes closed and clutching her injured arm. Dywana's mouth tightened as she grasped hold of the other side of the boat and helped Jago to pull it out of the water to the safety of dry land.

Gawain sat up and started to clamber over the side but Tamar remained where she was, on the boards of the boat with her knees pulled up to her chest. She cradled her injured arm, protecting it as best she could, while a muffled melody rose out of her pocket. The watch had finished playing the sea shanties and had started on a tune that both Jago and Dywana knew well.

It was a song of defiance and triumph against all odds; a song that all Cornish folk would recognise and, despite their worries, both Jago and Dywana found themselves humming the tune.

'A good sword and a trusty hand! A merry heart and true!'

As the watch continued to play Tamar said quietly, 'We learnt that at school.'

'Everyone in Cornwall learns that song,' Gawain remarked. Then, taking in Tamar's appearance properly for the first time, he added, 'Hey, you look terrible!'

'Thanks!' Tamar replied and closed her eyes again as another wave of nausea took hold.

Meanwhile, in a few deep words, Jago was describing to Dywana all that had happened during their rescue. Her face clouded as he recounted the woman's scream, summoning the memories from deep beneath the sea.

'She 'as no right to meddle with the memories of the past!' Dywana exclaimed out loud.

'She 'as no right to do any of the things she 'as done,' Jago replied grimly. 'But until the sword is in place, 'er power will go unchallenged. Everything lies in the hands of young Arthur.'

Dywana scrutinised the sea, with its now empty horizon. The storm had quietened and the first of the stars were just becoming visible. She wondered how far Arthur had got but he was well out of her range now.

Jago interrupted her thoughts, 'Come on lass, our work is here. These two need our attention.'

He leant into the boat and lifted Tamar over the side.

Together they walked towards the cottage, with Jago carrying Tamar, as Cathe emerged from the lane; nothing more than a normal, ginger, domestic cat. He stalked towards Gawain and with a great, rumbling purr rubbed against his legs, then he moved on to Jago and finally to Dywana.

She looked down at him, 'Do I take it then, that everyone is safe – at least for now?'

The purr increased in volume and both Jago and Dywana looked at one another and smiled.

'Well, that *is* good,' Dywana said. 'And we can tell Kitto and Morwenna that these two are safe.'

'But,' Jago answered, 'they must stay 'ere till the morning, they can be met then.'

He added a few deep words and Dywana listened before nodding gravely.

'It's not finished yet. I know Jago.'

At the edge of the beach, perched on a rock, the Writer sat with her bag by her side. She listened to the conversation and to the deep words and then glanced at the cliff above her to where the Watcher stood, waiting. She sent him a brief, silent command and he bowed once before turning and disappearing into the shadows.

The Writer turned her attention back to the scene on the beach and, not for the first time, Dywana felt her gaze and instantly they were in conversation, using their time-honoured language of deep words interwoven with purple and silver. Then the Writer picked up her bag and, with a tiny nod, turned and made her way off the beach towards one of the caves.

Once inside, she picked up an unlit lantern sitting on a rocky ledge. At her touch it burst into light, the flame steady despite the slight breeze which flowed through the cave. Tiny droplets of water fell from the roof and splashed into puddles on the cave bed. The Writer walked further into the hillside and on towards the other place where a King lay sleeping.

...

Dywana and Jago watched the Writer disappear into the cave before closing the cottage door, at which point a voice called out to them from the kitchen.

'Are they safe then?'

'Safe but hurt, Lance,' Dywana answered.

'Bring them here, where I may see them.'

'You've climbed out then?'

'Of course I've climbed out,' the voice replied irritably. 'But it's taken it out of me. I've been in there so long I'd forgotten the pull of gravity.'

Dywana pushed the kitchen door open. At the far end of the table an elderly man sat with his hands held protectively over a shield lying in front of him. His hair, eyebrows and beard were white. The painting that hung on the kitchen wall was hanging slightly askew and, whereas it had previously depicted a knight and his horse, now neither were visible.

'So, my great-nephew is on his way then?'

Dywana nodded, 'He is Lance.'

233

The old man grunted, 'He's a brave 'un.'

But then his attention was drawn to Gawain and to Tamar, still in Jago's arms.

'And so, by the looks of it, are you two.'

'Good to see you again, Lance,' Jago said, as he carefully deposited Tamar on a chair.

'And you my old friend,' Lance replied.

'I need to see to your arm, Tamar,' Dywana said, ignoring the two men. 'Can you roll your sleeve up?'

Tamar nodded and, biting her lip as the pain cut into her and trying not to retch, did as she was asked.

Dywana, disregarding the fact that her old friend had climbed out of a painting, started to bustle around the kitchen, pulling out bottles and bandages. At the same time she was reaching into cupboards, putting plates on the table and piling tins of cakes and biscuits in front of the men.

Then she stretched up to a shelf where an assortment of stone jars and dust-covered glass bottles were squeezed together, and selected a squat, green bottle. She pulled out the stopper and Tamar was overwhelmed with the scent of honey and roses, and the sound of bees buzzing. Arthur's aunt slowly tipped the bottle, allowing just a few drops to fall onto Tamar's injured arm.

As it left the bottle the liquid glistened, a rich, earthy brown, but the instant it touched Tamar's skin it changed to glossy gold. And straightaway Tamar felt the pain dull and, before she knew it, her arm was bound and in a sling.

Then Dywana turned to Gawain and lightly dropped a little of the liquid onto his head and the open wound, and immediately the blood was stilled. Her touch was really quite remarkable.

'We'll get you to the doctor Tamar, but it's already late an' you an' Gawain will be needed before the night's done.' She paused, 'D'you think you'll be alright?'

Tamar nodded. She was one of the Guardians, she *had* to be alright.

Dywana examined Tamar's face, the girl certainly looked a little better. The pocket watch chimed once, reminding them that Tamar was also the Time Keeper. There was no choice; Tamar had to be with the other three.

Then Arthur's aunt turned to the men. She looked Lance up and down and pushed one of the plates of food closer to him, but he shook his head.

'There's no time for eating, that may come later Dywana, but now I'm needed elsewhere.' He stood up, picked up his shield and retrieved a sword from under the kitchen table.

'You can't be goin' so soon!' Jago said.

'There's little time to spare, old friend. I would stay and talk but the stars beckon me.'

'Oh Lance!' Dywana exclaimed. 'Surely you're not really goin' already? You've hardly eaten a thing! An' you've been in that darn painting for so long that you must be as weak as a kitten.'

His face softened as he took in her expression. 'I have to go Dywana. Arthur's on his way and the others are gathering.'

And while checking that his sword was firmly in its scabbard, added, 'And me... weak as a kitten? One of our King's famous knights and a knight of the Round Table? Never!'

Dywana, appearing to ignore his protestations, merely asked, 'Well, are you comin' back?'

The old knight shook his head, 'I know not, m' dear.'

Horse's hooves echoed outside the cottage and Jago leant out of the window. 'Your horse 'as arrived, Lance,' he announced.

The elderly warrior nodded, picked up his cloak and flung it around his shoulders. Dywana's eyes followed her friend's every move as the old knight assembled his belongings.

Sighing she said, 'Well, Lance, I understand if that's how it 'as to be, but at least take something with you!' And delving deep into a drawer she pulled out a sheet of creased, brown paper and wrapped up a large slice of cherry cake.

'Here,' she said awkwardly, her eyes glistening as she offered him the food-parcel. 'You must be needin' *some* nourishment after so many years.'

The old knight smiled, his hooded eyes crinkling, and he leaned over to enfold Dywana in a crushing hug. 'With your cherry cake inside me I'll be as strong as an ox, Dywana.'

But at that moment thunder boomed above the cottage and a sudden flash of lightning lit up the room. It was a call to war.

Lance's smile disappeared, 'It seems that our allies and our enemies are assembling. I must be gone, they will be waiting at the lake.'

Dywana stood back, she knew he had to go but she couldn't bring herself to speak. She'd become so used to having conversations with the two-dimensional version of her friend that she couldn't imagine her kitchen without him. Lance made his way to the kitchen door but he faltered and, turning, looked at Gawain and Tamar.

'So much courage in such young hearts, Arthur has chosen his friends well.'

There was a tick from the clock, and the seal on the windowsill blinked as far-away chiming and singing drifted in from the open window. However the gravity of the moment was shattered as Lancelot broke into a broad, silver-bearded grin and said, 'Look after Dywana if I don't return Jago. She needs someone to organise!'

And with a clatter of armour, sword and shield, he was gone.

There was silence in the little cottage kitchen, and Dywana cleared her throat and dabbed her eyes with her shawl.

'Well,' she started, her voice coming out as a croak. 'Well!' she said again.

But Jago just took a couple of plates, piled them up and pushed them towards Tamar and Gawain as if nothing extraordinary had happened. Gawain thought of his uncle; Kitto Cornish would have revelled in the possibility of meeting a knight freshly released from a painting. And not just *any* knight, but a knight from King Arthur's court.

'You two must also be on your way very soon,' Jago stated, 'but you must try to eat somethin' first. Who knows 'ow long the night will be?'

'Yes, an' I'll tell you where you 'ave to wait,' Dywana added, collecting her thoughts and trying to concentrate on Tamar and Gawain's mission, rather than the loss of her kitchen-companion.

Making his way to the hall, Jago said, 'I'll phone Kitto and Morwenna an' tell them you're both safe an' sound an' stayin' here. They'll be able to tell everyone else and call off the search... an' the rest can wait till tomorrow.'

Tamar was immediately reminded of the night they'd been made Guardians. She remembered Bedivere and Angela ushering them out of the cottage when they'd only just returned from seeing Matearnas throw herself to her death. She was getting a touch of deja-vu.

. . .

Arthur sat astride Argo and watched the last of the memories flee past, and then he looked at Zephaniah at his side. Time should move forwards but it seemed that it could also flow backwards. He felt as though he was standing on a white line in the centre of a road with traffic driving either side of him in opposite directions.

Zephaniah rested his hand on Argo's neck, 'Ready then boy?'

Arthur almost answered but Argo got there first, his deep, horsey words feeding into his brain - so this is what it was like to be able to understand a horse. Although, Arthur thought, probably not every horse could master the deep words. He grinned as there was a whinny as Argo agreed with him.

Then the stallion turned and Arthur thought he heard him say, 'Are you ready, Sire?' before he began to trot and then gallop along the path. Together, the horse and his rider gathered speed until they were hurtling through the tunnel of trees towards the open moorland and the lake. And Arthur's destiny.

Chapter 21

~ The Lady of the Lake ~

Holding the lantern, the Writer walked deeper into the hillside, the path winding down through layers of rock. Along the way tiny niches were carved out of the grey stone. Each one held a candle, its flickering flame casting tall shadows across the roof of the tunnel. She looked behind her to see that Cathe had joined her and was keeping pace, quietly padding in her footsteps. She smiled at him and he purred in reply.

And as they walked the transformation began.

The Writer's dress, which had been a murky beige knee-length number, was lengthening and changing colour. Now stars of silver glinted and glistened on midnight-blue silk and the floor-length skirt swept the path with every step she took. Her hair, which had been steel-grey, released itself, snaking over her shoulders to fall glossy-black to her waist and the glasses disappeared. The Writer was finally herself.

Meanwhile the tunnel, which had begun its life as a modest opening at the back of the cave on Porth Talant beach, had widened to become a generous passage. Furthermore it had also become high enough to accommodate both a horse and his rider. In fact, judging by the hoof prints cast in the sandy floor, it might well have been used as a bridleway; although any rider would never have been a member of a pony club.

The woman and the cat had been walking along the tunnel for some time, and she knew that by now the stars would be out and the sky would be dark. The roof of the rocky way was dotted with silver points of light; an imitation of the Cornish night sky high above this underground path which would, even now, be wrapping itself around the legendary land.

The companions rounded a corner and a golden glow reached out towards them from an open doorway.

The Writer slowed down. Despite her calling and all that she had witnessed, she never failed to be moved by moments such as this. She checked the lantern and looked at Cathe striding beside her. He'd grown during their walk and was now at eye-level. They paused and together entered the chamber.

Carvings decorated the chamber walls, depicting knights in armour alongside their horses, and ladies in flowing dresses, all illuminated by eternally burning candles. The roof was a dome reaching high into the foundations of the hills. The floor was covered in layers of rugs, woven in deep reds, purple and gold; the colours of royalty.

The Writer approached the centre of the room and slowly climbed the stairs to a stone plinth where a man lay sleeping, dressed ready for battle.

Placing the lantern on the top step she bent over and whispered his name - and his eyes opened.

...

High on Cornwall's moors under a star-sprinkled sky, the lake was still, not even the tiniest of ripples disturbed the water's surface.

At the far side of the water, on the opposite bank, four figures waited and watched. One was a woman, dressed from head to toe in black and seated on a horse. Two men stood to her side. One had a crow on his shoulder and the other had long, pale hair and a white, albino hound at his feet. Slightly behind them, as if he didn't quite belong to the group, was a mounted rider wearing a cloak and a tricorn hat. The skeletal highwayman's skull gleamed in the moonlight and his bone-white fingers flexed and twitched.

Arthur looked at them with a sinking heart.

They were the reception committee from hell.

This doesn't look good,' Arthur said quietly to himself.

Out of the corner of his mouth, Zephaniah whispered, 'The devil's own they be.'

'Thanks,' Arthur replied. 'Maybe you and Nick should get together. He always knows how to make a situation a little bit better too!' It was only later that it occurred to him that suggesting Nick get together with a self-assembly memory was perhaps one of his more bizarre ideas.

Arthur was contemplating the strength of the opposition when he caught a movement out of the corner of his eye.

He swung around wondering what new horror could be approaching, but his heart leapt as he recognised who had come to join them.

It was Bedivere. He'd ridden up behind him and was now drawing level.

'Bedivere!'

However a whinny on his other side cut short the opportunity for further conversation, and Arthur spun around only to be confronted by his, supposedly-dead, great-uncle. Lance Penhaligon was also seated on a horse, dressed in armour and carrying a shield; in fact exactly as he'd been depicted in a painting, hanging on a kitchen wall.

And again all Arthur managed to say was his uncle's name, 'Great-Uncle Lance!'

The rider smiled, his eyes twinkling, 'Ah, my dear boy. We've at last been permitted to meet.'

Arthur stared.

The last time he'd met his great-uncle he'd been a tiny boy, and the way his parents had talked he'd assumed that he must have died. But of course, he'd heard him speaking from the painting in Dywana's kitchen! He wasn't sure whether that made his great-uncle dead or alive but, judging from the others waiting around the lake, that wasn't too unusual.

Lance nudged his horse forward and, leaning over, laid a hand on Arthur's shoulder, 'From what I hear you've fulfilled all our expectations. I'm proud of you lad. My nephew and his wife would be too – if they knew.'

And instantly Arthur had an alarming picture of his great-uncle riding in full armour down Castle Close to greet his parents.

His dad would die of heart failure.

'Um, well, it's probably just as well they don't,' Arthur replied. 'But thanks anyway!'

Lance chuckled but then his laughter died away and a silence, deeper than any silence Arthur had ever known, fell on those waiting at the lake side.

Two figures, one carrying a lantern and wearing a dress which shimmered with every step, had emerged from a fold in the hills and were walking towards the lake - accompanied by a green-eyed black cat. The animal was enormous, as big as any man, and Arthur thought that he caught snatches of deep conversation exchanged between Argo and the creature.

Slowly, both the ancient knights dismounted and made their way towards the trio. As they approached the lady and her dark-haired companion they bent and knelt - and Arthur remembered. This was the boy-man who'd appeared to him on the hill a year ago, giving him instructions and help when he'd most needed it. The one who'd called him Art.

It was then that he heard the words – and straightaway he was sliding off his horse and following the two old knights and kneeling before this almost-stranger. A hand on his head and Arthur was filled with the peace that he'd last felt on the hillside that summer night as the sword had touched his shoulder.

'Art, you've done well,' a deep voice said, and Arthur could hear the smile as its owner added, 'you are a true knight.'

'You see now Sire, I told you he'd be The One,' Lance said. 'I could see it even when he was a baby.'

'Lancelot - as ever – you're right.'

'Art, you must stand, I cannot have you kneel!' the man was saying and smiled. 'You know who I am?'

Arthur nodded as he got to his feet. His gaze took in the man's armour which, even in the moonlight, shone, and he took a deep breath before acknowledging what he'd known all along. Slowly he lifted his eyes to meet those of the man standing in front of him, and said, 'You're King Arthur.'

At these words the King's smile broadened and his eyes twinkled, 'Well said, Art.'

Then he turned to the old knights, 'A worthy choice. I've been told of Art's bravery, but his perception marks him out as The One who must follow on. It is true that courage will be necessary, but insight and intelligence will be his most useful gifts.'

Both the knights nodded gravely in agreement but the Writer smiled at Arthur reassuringly, which was as well because Arthur was feeling a distinct lack of any of the qualities which King Arthur had listed.

The King continued, 'And, Art, you know your destiny?'

Again - although a little more hesitantly - Arthur nodded.

'That is good,' King Arthur said, but then he looked across the lake and his smile disappeared to be replaced by a frown.

'We have company, but this is neither the time nor the place for battle. They are mistaken if they think that the prize can be taken here. There will be other occasions for their desire for blood to be satisfied, but now is not the time.'

'Come,' he said beckoning to Arthur, and strode to the edge of the lake. A boat sat moored, waiting, and Arthur obediently followed his name-sake with more than a little nervousness.

'T'is your time, Art, mine is done. You are the one who must claim the sword.'

The legendary King was gesturing to the boat and Arthur realised that he was meant to get in. He hoped it didn't rock too much because he wasn't brilliant in boats, and he wasn't too keen on adding 'clumsy' to his list of talents. He climbed in and looked for the oars but there weren't any, and then there was the slightest jolt and the boat began to move. No motor, no oars, no sails, but still it glided out into the calm, mirror-perfect lake.

Arthur clung to the sides wondering what would happen next. He glanced at those waiting at the lake's edge, and caught sight of John Oliver standing with

Michael and Angela Jolly. He hadn't seen Angela since that night a year ago when he'd been made Guide, chief of the Guardians. He wondered what she'd been doing when Michael had been in Pendrym, but the boat was slowing, gliding to a halt, and Arthur concentrated on what was happening in front of him.

A tiny ripple was spreading out from a point in the centre of the lake. He leaned forward. Something was rising, glinting, out of the water. It was the tip of a sword. Slowly it emerged, rising higher until its hilt became visible – held by a pale hand; a woman's hand.

Another piece of the jigsaw fell into place as Arthur remembered the legend of the Lady of the Lake. In the story Sir Bedivere had carried Excalibur to the Lady for safe-keeping. Only now it was more than a story. Or if it was a story - he was in it.

It was then that he heard the deep, golden words spoken by the Lady of the Lake.

'Art, you are the Appointed One, the Chosen One.

The sword is yours.

Yours for the protection of our fair land.

You must take it and use it; but only ever use it for good.

Claim it now as yours.'

The hand raised the sword higher and Arthur leant towards it and grasped the hilt. He looked down into the water. Large pale eyes looked up at him in a face framed by long ribbons of silver hair. The Lady was beautiful, in a sort of watery way, and smiled at him. Then he was taking the hilt of the sword and it was as he'd remembered; a perfect fit. The pale hand disappeared beneath the waters, leaving Arthur holding the sword - his sword. He lifted it, once more marvelling at the intricate engravings and jewels.

He turned towards those waiting for him and lifted the sword high for them to see as the boat carried him back across the lake and towards the shore. Reaching land it stopped so gently that it didn't even rock. Arthur climbed over the side carrying the sword in one hand, not the easiest of manoeuvres, and looked towards those waiting for him.

His supporters had gathered together on the little sandy beach, ready to greet him, but the one he regarded was Excalibur's previous owner. This man stood flanked by Lance and Bedivere and as Arthur set foot on the shore he stepped forward.

'Art,' he said, 'the Lady has proclaimed you as Lord of this land. This is your time - and the sword is now your sword.'

He glanced at the two elderly knights, 'Gentlemen and knights, you are my witnesses that the power formerly entrusted to me has now been passed to my heir, Arthur Penhaligon.'

Both knights nodded solemnly.

'And your allegiance must lie with him, for as long as you shall live.'

Again they nodded but Arthur saw a cloud pass across their faces. This other King had been their leader for more than a lifetime, many lifetimes, and yet here he was instructing them to take Arthur Penhaligon as their chief.

Their former King smiled, 'Art, these men will become accustomed to following you as Cornwall's crowned leader; and if you can allow for Lance always being right and Bedivere talking in riddles, all will be well.'

He scanned the motley group headed by the woman on horseback, waiting on the opposite side of the lake, and muttered under his breath, 'And gentlemen, your first task will be to ensure Art's safe exit from this place. I leave that in your hands.'

He embraced Bedivere and Lancelot, talking quietly to them and giving them further instructions, before smiling and saying, 'Friends, we will meet again and that meeting will not be tinged with sadness. It will be filled with joy. '

Finally he turned to Arthur.

'Art, you have been Chosen. Your path will not always be easy but you will never have to tread it alone.'

He rested his hand on Arthur's shoulder and, raising his voice so that everyone could hear, said, 'Art, You are the Chosen One, you are now more than a Guardian or the Guide. You are The One appointed to carry Cornwall's crown. Art you are Cornwall's King. Go - protect her!' And with these words he turned and nodded to the Writer.

Arthur watched as she held up the lamp and its perpetually burning candle. He saw the affectionate glances sent towards the knights by their much-loved King and questioned how his own leadership could possibly replace that of such a brave and fearless man. But he waited with Excalibur in his hand as, with the Writer on one side and Cathe on the other, the fabled King disappeared once more into the folds of the hills and deep into Cornwall's heart.

. . .

Viatoris, the Watcher, had witnessed the entire ceremony from his vantage-point above the lake. He'd Watched the responsibility for Cornwall's care pass from man to boy. He'd felt young Arthur's doubts in his own ability to step into the great man's shoes, and he'd observed the ancient knights and their sadness as they made their farewells to the man they'd known so well and for so long. But he also knew that both Lancelot and Bedivere were loyal and trustworthy. It was without question that they would do whatever was requested of them for Cornwall and their new King. Viatoris monitored the progress of the stately procession of the once-King, Cathe and the Writer to the waiting hillside, and marked the moment when the lamp-light disappeared. He was a Watcher, he had seen many wonderful and terrible things, but this was perhaps one of the most touching events that he'd had the honour to witness. With a sigh, and a slight pang of regret, he turned his attention back towards the lake and waited for what he knew must come next.

He grimaced as a murderous scream shattered the peace. The Lady of Darkness was summoning her followers to battle, sending out a call to creatures and men to avenge the blood of Matearnas and to align themselves with her - Cornwall's rightful queen.

And in the blink of an eye the sky was filled with a storm of bats, swooping and diving towards the group on the lakeside beach. Unformed bodies or parts of bodies, swarmed out of the granite hills and, with a howl, the white hound at the Crow Man's side sped around the lake intent on reaching Arthur.

And then it was a blur of horses' hooves, raised swords, shouts and cries, barks, yelping and frenzied commands. He saw Arthur raise his sword and heard Bedivere's shouted instruction, 'Go Art. Take the sword and go!'

He saw Arthur hesitate, torn between staying to fight alongside his people and the knowledge of what he still had to do. And it was with some relief that Viatoris saw the boy come to a decision and quickly pull himself onto Argo's high back. He Watched as the horse reared up with the boy brandishing that famous sword in his right hand and he heard Arthur's shout of, 'For Cornwall!' as the horse wheeled around and galloped from the lake with Lightning at its side. He saw them disappear towards the coast, pursued by a skeletal highwayman - and a hound from hell.

Chapter 22

~ Battle ~

Gawain and Tamar approached the gate and looked at each other.

'Are you sure we're meant to come here?' Tamar asked.

He nodded and slowly opened the gate. The light from the full moon was just enough to make out the gravelled path winding through the graves.

Long shadows stretched across the path, unfurling from the feet of the granite tombstones marking the final resting place of the yard's inhabitants. Mossy crosses and ornate statues mingled with simple stones. Hardly a blade of grass or a leaf of a tree moved, and the only sound was the gentle swish of the sea from Porth Talant beach far below.

'Creepy,' Tamar whispered.

Gawain didn't reply because he had the sense of someone near-by listening in to their conversation.

A tiny shape darted across their path and Tamar started. She wasn't certain that she could handle any more surprises, she felt that she'd had enough to last a lifetime. She sidled closer to Gawain - she didn't care if he thought she was a wimp.

'Why did we have to come here?' she asked.

'Don't know, but there'll be a reason,' he replied, and put his arm around her. She didn't make any protest and it made him feel better too.

The path curled around and up through the graveyard and past the dark mass of the church. The gravel crunched under their feet, heralding their entrance to anyone who might be lying in wait for them and Gawain felt, rather than saw, a movement out of the corner of his eye.

He stopped and stared into the gloom. Where a moment before he could have sworn he'd seen a shadow move, suddenly there was nothing. The Watcher had stepped back into the deeper shadows.

'This is horrible!' Tamar whispered.

'I know', Gawain said. 'But Dywana said that we had to wait at the edge of the graveyard overlooking Porth Talant bay.'

As he said this a shape among the tombstones moved. It detached itself from the stones and a familiar voice ordered, 'Go boy!'

And a creature was flying towards them, it was about the size of a rat – with wings, and it was breathing fire.

'It's Dragon!' Gawain exclaimed.

Tamar was still clutching his arm.

She heard the relief in his voice but couldn't quite equate it with being attacked by a tiny, fire-breathing dragon.

And then a realisation hit her; it was exactly the same as the model Nick had found on the path. The last time she'd seen it the creature had been nothing more than green stone - and now here it was flying at her! A real, live, flying dragon made of blood, fire and scales.

'What - that can't be the thing Nick found!'

Gawain chuckled, realising that the figure among the graves was their friend. 'Think they might both be insulted if you call Dragon a 'thing'!'

The dragon flew past at eye level, executed a perfect loop, and flew back to his master.

'Guys!' the figure said, moving away from a monument of a stone angel. 'Am I glad to see you!'

'Nick,' Tamar exclaimed, diving towards him, only remembering her injured arm at the last minute.

'Ow!' she shouted, as he pulled her into an immense hug. 'Careful... my arm.'

Gawain slapped his friend on the back, 'Mate, it's good to see you.'

For a few seconds they just stood and grinned at one another before Nick caught sight of Gawain's head which, even in the moonlight, still looked a mess.

His grin disappeared, 'Was that... ?'

Gawain nodded, 'Our very good friend, the Crow Man.'

'Man, he's evil.'

'Sure is!'

'And that?' Nick asked, pointing to Tamar's arm.

'One of the Crow Man's mates,' she said simply.

But the dragon, which had just landed on Nick's shoulder, was far more interesting to Tamar than her arm.

'He's so cute! A real dragon - he can't be the same one you found on the path, can he?'

Nick nodded. 'Yeah, he is. Gawain was there when he began to come to life.'

Bored by the chatter, the dragon's attention was diverted by a moth. He snapped at it - flames shooting out of his jaws - and the moth became a char-grilled snack.

'Quick too,' Tamar remarked, impressed. 'That's so cool; imagine having your very own dragon. How did he, um, stop being stone?'

But the explanation would have to wait because, in the corner of Tamar's pocket, the watch was stirring. It cranked its cogs, it could feel the images forming, and whirring and spinning it set to work, chiming to announce their creation.

Nick watched, intrigued, as Tamar extracted a beautiful pocket watch from her jeans.

The instant the watch was opened it lit up and images began to appear, flickering and dancing across its face. Tamar wondered if she'd see Zephaniah again, but this time it wasn't a street scene but individual pictures.

The first picture the watch showed them was a cruel face, partially hidden by a mask.

Then the clock chimed once more and the flesh fell away, leaving a masked skull, and Nick exclaimed, 'I know him!'

'You know a *skeleton*?' Gawain asked incredulously.

'Yeah, he was here.'

'Here?'

But the clock chimed again, halting Nick's explanation, and they watched as the skull was replaced by a sword rising out of water.

Another chime and another image; of a woman carrying a lamp deep into a hillside.

Chime – the woman disappeared and they were watching two knights on horseback galloping across open moorland.

Chime - a boy riding a white stallion with a sword in his hand. They all recognised the boy. It was Arthur.

Then the chiming stopped and the images faded, leaving an ordinary clock face. However, just as the pictures disappeared Tamar caught a glimpse of a woman dressed from head to toe in velvet, riding a black horse.

And it was this image, out of all of them, which disturbed her most.

It was then that they heard the hooves.

...

Arthur had obeyed Bedivere's instruction and set his face towards the coast. Deep words had come at him from all sides, some were dark black or dingy grey, inflicting agony, but others were warm and encouraging. Among the beautiful silver and gold of the positive words, he'd heard Michael and Angela's instructions and those of the old knights. There were other voices, but they all said the same thing, 'Go!'

And although it had torn him in two, Arthur knew that his duty was to take the sword to the one who waited.

So, digging his heels into the stallion's side, he shouted his pledge to his homeland and then said, 'It's you and me Argo, let's get out of here. You know where we've got to go.'

Together they sped over the moors towards the Smugglers' Way. Argo galloped, flying across the open moorland and gaining speed with every stride until the night-cloaked land became a blur.

Arthur had never ridden bare-back but, with one hand threaded through Argo's mane and the other clutching the sword, somehow he remained seated as they wove between rocks and mossy boulders and raced into the tree-tunnel towards the coast.

The moon shone down on the horse and the boy, fleeing down the ancient path and mingling with the memories. Flashes of faces, glimpses of frock-coats, an ankle here, a gloved hand there, joined him in their desperation to escape the evil at their backs.

However it wasn't long before Arthur felt, then heard, the hooves galloping behind him and he didn't need to look to find out who was chasing them. He felt every deep and dark word which the highwayman sent slicing through his brain because, after all, the skeleton was an expert in the art of inflicting pain - he'd had centuries to polish his skill.

Arthur tried to block the barrage of words and instead to concentrate on the ride and on his quest. He'd come this far and he was determined to live up to the trust the King had placed in him. No bag of bones was going to prevent him from achieving his goal. Arthur glanced down at Lightning running at Argo's side, the dog was living up to his name, and then sent a brief word of thanks to the horse.

The reply was a breathless whinny.

The path opened up ahead of them and already they were approaching the sea and Arthur could smell the salt in the air. And now they were in a lane. Trees, fields and hedges passed in a flash of an eye but, little by little, their hunter was gaining on them.

. . .

Servo, the Watcher, had arrived at the churchyard above Porth Talant bay shortly before Gawain and Tamar. He'd felt Gawain's awareness of his presence and was impressed, that must mean that the boy must be one of the rare ones who could see beyond the visible world – a rare and precious gift. He'd smiled at the delight of the three Guardians meeting one another and at Tamar's enchantment with the tiny green-stone dragon. He'd been just as intrigued as the boys were by the clock entrusted to the Time Keeper and by the images it had showed the three Guardians. However the drumming hoof beats drawing close to the coast signalled another chapter in the unfolding story taking place in front of him, and he turned towards the wooden gate and Watched.

A stallion burst through the gate, the boy still clinging to his back and the dog at his side. He saw a white hound bound after them, up the gravelled path and through the graves. He Watched the highwayman on his mount and saw the horse buck and rear at the entrance to the churchyard. He heard the words as the skeleton slid from the horse's back and ran, bones jangling, in pursuit of the boy and his prize.

He looked up to the skies as the thunder clouds rolled in and the lightning crackled above them – and he heard the cries of the memories in the bay below them. He frowned. He knew what he would see, those long-dead, long-drowned souls, crying out for help. The Lady of Darkness was summoning every memory, disturbing this ancient land in her bid for power.

Nick was the first to react as he shouted, 'Go get him boy!' and launched the dragon towards the white hound.

Dragon took off, soared vertically upwards, performed an aerial somersault and plunged back down towards his target. A second later there was a jet of flame, a yelp, a howl, and the scent of burning fur. Dragon had hit the mark and was already after his next prey.

Arthur galloped towards the cliff edge but turning, he saw the highwayman just paces behind him. There was nowhere to go. Excalibur in his hand he jumped from Argo's back. This was one battle he was determined to fight.

'Over here!' Arthur commanded, calling Nick and Gawain to his side.

He lifted the sword with both hands, ready to bring it crashing down onto the highwayman's skull just as the skeleton raised his pistol.

'Look out!' Gawain cried, diving forwards.

A, 'crack', the scent of gunpowder and the sound of screams and shouts filled the air. The churchyard was a confusion of moonlit bodies, snapping jaws, glinting metal and fire. Dragon launched himself again, a fiery rocket, while Lightning concentrated on wreaking revenge on his opposite number. Blood flowed, black and white fur flew, and razor-sharp teeth bit into soft flesh.

Tamar watched the whirling mass of animal and human bodies, she was desperate to join in but the pocket watch had showed her that this wasn't her battle. Her fight was with someone else and it was one she had to face alone.

Argo stood waiting for her beside a stone monument.

Muttering a quiet, 'sorry', to anyone who might hear, she ran to the horse and clambered on to the stone at his side. From there, wrapping her good arm around his neck, she pulled herself on to his back. The instant that she was seated he took off, cantering back down the path towards the lane and carrying her towards her enemy.

The boys were vaguely aware of Argo's departure. Arthur heard Tamar's muted apology but at that moment he was thrown sideways and a burning pain seared his shoulder.

The sword lunged forwards, almost of its own accord, ripping the highwayman's cloak and plunging between his ribs to where his heart had once been.

. . .

In the lane outside the churchyard Tamar sat mounted on the white stallion, waiting.

She heard the shouts of battle from among the graves and saw the sky lit by Dragon's flames. She heard the barks and yelps and wondered if Lightning would be able to defeat the hell-hound.

It was then that she heard those other hooves and said to herself, 'I hope that this is what I was meant to do.'

And sure enough, true to the picture in the pocket watch, a ramrod-straight figure wearing black velvet and riding a wide-eyed horse rounded the bend in the lane.

Words, sending shivers down Tamar's spine, floated towards her, 'So, the girl waits alone.'

It was the woman, the Lady of Clehy. She whipped her horse, drawing blood from the beast's side, and trotted up the lane towards Tamar and Argo.

'Do you believe this to be a wise choice?' she asked, mockingly.

Tamar said nothing, she could feel her heart drumming in her chest. She *really* hoped that she'd got it right.

The woman halted her horse with a sharp pull on the reins. The animal whinnied in pain and danced sideways, Argo shifted and Tamar felt his anger.

At least the woman was alone and not accompanied by either of her henchmen, the Crow Man or the Pale Guy, Tamar thought, as she tried to still her shaking hands.

Clearing her throat Tamar found her voice, but instead of coming out as she wanted, sounding brave and strong, there was a distinct quiver to it. 'You know that you'll never win don't you?' She took a deep breath, willing her voice to be steady, 'Arthur is the One who's been Chosen – not you.'

But Tamar's adversary merely threw her head back and laughed, 'Oh, listen to the girl. She thinks that I, the Lady of Clehy, can be defeated by a mere boy.'

Then she stopped laughing, tilted her head and studied Tamar thoughtfully. She mused, 'Such courage in one so young – what a waste!'

The Lady of Clehy nudged her horse forwards until they were within a couple of paces of each other.

She whispered, 'Do you not remember my touch, girl? I have more power in one, tiny finger than all of you between you.'

Tamar sat on Argo, biding her time, waiting for the right moment and for the shaking to stop. She was almost close enough.

The woman continued, 'The sword is mine, as is Cornwall. Matearnas may have failed but I will succeed. I will rule.'

She smiled, lifted her hand and the thunder boomed.

'You see? There really is no point to this self-sacrifice you mistake for bravery. The power is already mine.'

Tamar looked at the distance between them; would it work? If she left it any longer the woman may get too close. Argo neighed softly and, taking several deep breaths in an effort to still her rapidly beating heart, she took his advice.

Slowly, Tamar reached into her pocket.

'Your power may seem strong but it's nothing compared to the power we've been entrusted with,' she started, her voice becoming stronger. 'Your mistake is to believe in yourself, as if the power is yours. It isn't.

Nor is the power we've been given. None of it's ours; it's just a gift – like this!'

And, as a magician might pull a rabbit out of a hat, Tamar pulled out the pocket-watch given to her as Time Keeper. She flipped it open and the air was filled with light and music. The effect on the woman was instant.

'No!' she whispered, her voice hoarse.

The watch started playing Trelawney's song; the Cornish song of defiance and rebellion. The song of a proud and ancient people.

Tamar held the watch up and nudged Argo forwards. The woman drew back and now she was the one who was shaking. Then there was a growl, and paws as large as dinner plates padded down the lane to stand beside Argo. Tamar glanced at the cat that had arrived at her side and did a double-take. He was huge. His gaze met hers and she immediately understood that he was implying that she should concentrate on the matter in hand. Obediently, but with her mind performing somersaults, she closed her mouth and turned back to the woman.

'You know what happens when this touches you, don't you?' Tamar asked, because the watch's role had become clear to her. 'You'll be sent back to your own time and place, and I'm pretty sure that you'll be dead in ours.'

On cue, the clock chimed once and the woman's skin started to sag and her blond hair became grey. The Lady of Darkness looked down at her hands, ageing in front of her; transparent flesh and dark veins were taking the place of youthful skin. She looked back to the pocket watch, its light glowing in the darkness. The longer she stayed close to it, the older she became.

Tamar was about to nudge Argo forwards, to press home her advantage, when the atmosphere around her rippled.

She glanced towards the churchyard just as Matearnas' hound burst, yelping, through the gate. It had been defeated by a black and white dog - and a dragon. And in that moment the woman turned her horse and was galloping down the lane as if her life depended on it which, in a way, it did.

Tamar dug her heels into Argo but he wouldn't move. Neither did the cat at her side.

'What!' Tamar exclaimed.

Instead Argo turned back towards the churchyard and the cat started to rumble, its purr an engine ticking over, and growled softly. And Tamar understood that she had to let the woman go, this time anyway. She glanced back down the lane, but both the hound and the woman had gone, and then she realised that the light in the sky was intensifying and that Argo was carrying her back up the path and past the church towards her friends. She flicked her hair out of her eyes and looked at the tableau set out in front of her.

. . .

Afterwards Nick and Arthur would always dispute who had been the true victor. Nick forever maintained that if it hadn't been for Dragon, Arthur would never have completed his quest. While Arthur clung to that moment when Excalibur had sunk into his bony rival and the skeleton had literally fallen apart, leaving nothing more than a heap of bleached bones topped by a cloak and a burnt tricorn hat. However both of them knew that the true hero had been Gawain, diving in front of his friend and knocking him out of the path of the shot aimed at Arthur's heart, so that the shot which had been intended to kill him had merely grazed his shoulder.

Maybe it *was* a team effort which enabled Arthur to secure the goal. Perhaps Nick's words, spoken on a moonlit hill a year before, had become reality and they truly had become like the Musketeers who'd lived centuries before. However the last part of the quest had to be accomplished by Arthur alone.

So it was the young boy-king who carried the sword to the waiting hand while trying to ignore the pain digging down through his shoulder. It was Arthur Penhaligon who, all too aware that the skeleton wasn't alone in his bid to seize Excalibur, finally staggered towards the stone angel and gritting his teeth, lifted the sword to fulfil his quest.

And Tamar, riding Argo up the moonlit path, was just in time to witness Arthur slip the sword into the sculpted stone hand. She felt the earth judder as a zigzag of underground thunder spread out from the angel towards every corner of Cornwall, announcing the victory of light over dark. And she saw the newly appointed King, accompanied by his friends, turn to face her.

What they saw was a girl, pale-faced and dark-eyed, with one arm in a sling and seated on a white stallion - escorted by an immense black cat.

As she approached the boys she simply said, 'I'll explain later.'

Then she focused on Arthur, and the blood seeping from his shoulder, and added, 'Looks like Dywana's got more work to do.'

Arthur looked at her; she seemed different. There was something about her that he hadn't noticed before but Nick, catching the look passing between them, nudged Gawain and grinned. The seconds ticked by until Arthur suddenly became aware of Nick's scrutiny.

He gathered himself as he regarded the clear, night sky and the sword now safely in the angel's hand, and exclaimed, 'Hey guys, we did it!'

Gawain nodded and added, 'Yeah… well us and Dragon.'

'Too right!' Nick agreed proudly.

But their conversation dwindled as they noticed that the sword had begun to shine and that something was happening in the bay below them, because now the sword's touch was reaching into Cornwall's waters. Dolphins swam and leapt through the peaceful sea, and a lone seal slipped silently below the waves. The memories had been stilled, at last allowed to rest as Excalibur's power in the angel's hand was spreading out, covering Cornwall - and her seas.

Beyond Lemayne Island, wood splintered and a mast cracked. Sails were torn and shredded and slowly a ship started to list sideways. A boy, the only crew left on board, looked above him at the masts now keeling over and said, 'I knew it! They left me 'ere on purpose. They must 'ave known this would 'appen,' and he dived into the sea. A few minutes later all that was left of the ship were a few timbers floating on the water's surface.

On Cornwall's moors, beside the silvery lake, Viatoris listened. He heard the rumble and felt the ground sing. He Watched as the sky and stars pulsed in harmony with the sword. Peace washed in waves, spreading out from Porth Talant and covering Cornwall from head to toe.

The Watcher observed those remaining at the lakeside and witnessed the cheering and manly backslapping among some and hugs between others. But sweeping the moorland for evidence of the Crow Man or Hagarawall, his pale-haired conspirator, he realised that both had disappeared. He wondered when, and how, they'd reappear, because he knew they would. Given time to lick their wounds, they would be determined to drag the power out of the hands of the newly appointed King and his allies.

However the Watcher wasn't given the luxury of a moment's more contemplation. He was being called back to Italy and the young Leonardo. He glanced towards Michael, caught up in the celebrations, and a deep thought was sent slamming into his skull.

'In future,' Michael said, 'leave the boy, Leonardo, in his own time.'

So Michael had seen them on the beach, but the next words Michael sent reassured him - apparently history hadn't been harmed. There was the unmistakable sound of a chuckle and if the Watcher had been close enough he might even have seen a hint of a twinkle in Michael's eye.

A second later, a *'woomph'*, and Viatoris was five hundred years away in Italy, Watching a small boy, called Leonardo Da Vinci, scribble pictures of a man doing the impossible. Flying.

...

And now -

The Writer standing at the cave's entrance looks up towards those silhouetted on the hillside above the bay; the new King and Cornwall's Guardians.

She turns to the knights waiting beside her.

'Cornwall has her King and her Guardians. And Excalibur is home. I will be asking you to retrieve the sword when the time is right. It will soon be needed at another place but, for now, Cornwall is safe.'

Lancelot and Bedivere standing tall and straight, glance at one another.

Then Lancelot grins and winks at Bedivere, 'Just like old times my friend!'

In a cave deep inside a hillside, a dark-haired man is shown a glimpse of his loyal friends and, smiling, lies down to sleep.

. . .

The pocket watch ticks contentedly, the cogs whirring in perfect harmony, happily united with the Time Keeper. It knows that they'll be going places together.

The dragon curls himself around Nick's neck, a green, scaly scarf. It snores, whirls of blue-grey smoke rising up, curling around his master's head. A claw contracts and his tail twitches. He's dreaming of chasing moths and a bony highwayman.

And in a dusty corner of a bedroom, a book flips wide open. Its pages turn, a blur of ink, until they slow and stop. A picture of a magical island, crowned by a castle and encircled by ice, illuminate the empty room.

The book – and the island – wait.

Dear Reader,

It's my dream that you've enjoyed reading this story as much as I enjoyed writing it.

I'm always delighted to hear from my readers; to find out which character they liked, or to discover which part of the story was their favourite, so I've included some of the places you can contact me near the back of the book. Please do write.

And, if you've got time, it would be great if you could post a review on Amazon or Goodreads. It would turn a fairly ordinary day into a very special day.

Thank you,
Rosie

A few notes and meanings.

The first book, 'The Golden Sword' (The Camelot Inheritance – Book 1), is also illustrated and published in both paperback and on kindle.

The third in 'The Camelot Inheritance' series will be published, complete with illustrations, in 2015.

You can follow my progress on Facebook: Rosie-Morgan-Cornwall

Or my blog: Rosie-Morgan-Cornwall.blogspot.com

Or on twitter: @WritingRosie

...

If you'd like to find out about some of the places in 'The Time Smugglers' here are their real names. (Maybe you'll come and visit Cornwall. If you do I think you might find them just as magical as the story.)

Porth Pyra is Polperro

Porth Talant is Talland Bay

Pendrym is Looe

All three names have their roots in the past or the Cornish language. For instance the manor of Pendrym, the area now known as East Looe, dates back to William the Conqueror's time – around 1066!

The Smuggler's Way is the name of a path leading inland from Polperro to the village of Pelynt, where I spent many happy years teaching some wonderful children. (I still think of you although now you'll all be adults!)

You will have noticed a few words spoken in Cornish in this story.

Cornish is an ancient Celtic language and is once again becoming popular. I'm proud to say that we even have road signs in Cornish as well as English.

These are most of the Cornish words I've used in 'The Camelot Inheritance' series so far:

Kernow = Cornwall
Matearnas = Queen
Brane = crow
Hagarawall = storm
Cathe = cat
Morah = one dolphin; morahas for more than one.
Na rewh nakevy = Don't forget
Comero weeth = Take care
Tereba nessa = Till next time
Durdathawhy = Good day
Theram cara Kernow = I love Cornwall
Clehy = ice
Taran = thunder
The labels on Dywana's bottles:
Agroas = rose-hips
Aiglets = hawthorn berries
Kevrin = secret
Medhegneth = medicine

Also, 'proper job', means something that's good, or has been done well. And 'dreckly', means sometime in the future and, being in Cornwall, it doesn't have to mean now!

The Watchers' names are Latin, an ancient language. Viatoris, who Watches the young Leonardo Da Vinci, means traveller, and Servo means to watch over or observe.

There have been sightings of a wild animal on the moor. It's thought that it is some sort of big cat, known as the Beast of Bodmin Moor. You might have guessed by now that Cathe is loosely based on the Beast.

Should you come to our beautiful county and explore the moors, always respect the fences around the disused mine shafts and take notice of any warning signs.

The song which the pocket watch was chiming is called Trelawney's song, there's quite a history to it, if you want to know more this is the title:

Trelawney's Song or 'The Song of the Western Men'

Acknowledgements

My thanks to Sigma Press for their kind permission to reference Craig Weatherhill's book, 'Cornish Place Names and Languages'.

To Andrew and Tricia, for your eagle-eyed proof-reading skills – and immense kindness.

My family and friends have been amazing in their support and encouragement. Thank you all *so* much. We all need people to believe in us.

But most of all, as ever, to Peter, my legendary, guitar-playing, science-teacher husband – who has been so understanding of my need to write; for knowing I'd go stir-crazy without it. You really are a legend!

About Rosie Morgan

Rosie lives, writes and draws in Cornwall, UK, where she shares her house with Pete and their two attention-seeking cats.

She's got a growing family and is ridiculously proud of all of them, young and old.

Once upon a time she used to teach.

Some of the schools were tiny, with two classrooms and an outdoor toilet (as well as resident spiders). Others were much bigger with rather more weather-proof, and cobweb-free, facilities. But all the schools had one thing in common, children; lots of them.

And each one of them was unique and talented in their own, very individual, way.

It's with these children in mind that Rosie writes her books and draws her pictures.

Printed in Great Britain
by Amazon.co.uk, Ltd.,
Marston Gate.